Damon kep[t] as he softly kissed her [...] cap- tivated. By everything about her. She was all red velvet and silken gold skin and everything he had ever wanted without knowing he wanted it. He didn't want to ever let her go. And if he had anything to say about it, he wouldn't. He took her face in his hands and stared down at her.

She sighed sweetly. "I was born to kiss you." She pressed her lips to his face, his mouth, his neck.

Inexplicably this beautiful woman had come into his life. Inexplicably, instantly, forcefully, he had fallen in love with her. With hardly a thought he had taken a risk and gone with it. But right from the beginning he had known there would be consequences for his actions, and now he had to face them.

He ran his hand through his hair. "Faith, I have a confession to make."

She knelt on the bed to be closer to him. "Don't be afraid. You can tell me anything. It's all right, this is our destiny."

She gently pressed her lips to his, but he couldn't keep the kiss light. She was everything he'd ever wanted. Driven by an uncontrollable need, he deepened the kiss. The depth of what he was feeling for her staggered him, the power of what he felt astounded him. But before he could have her completely, there was something he had to tell her . . . .

Only You

A novel by
Fayrene Preston

Based on the
screenplay written
by Diane Drake

BANTAM BOOKS
NEW YORK · TORONTO · LONDON · SYDNEY · AUCKLAND

ONLY YOU

A Bantam Book / October 1994

ISBN 0-553-56928-7

Published simultaneously in the United States and Canada

Bantam Books are published by Bantam Books, a division of Bantam Doubleday Dell
Publishing Group, Inc. Its trademark, consisting of the words "Bantam Books" and
the portrayal of a rooster, is Registered in U.S. Patent and Trademark Office and in
other countries. Marca Registrada. Bantam Books, 1540 Broadway, New York, New
York 10036.

PRINTED IN THE UNITED STATES OF AMERICA

OPM   0 9 8 7 6 5 4 3 2 1

Only You

PROLOGUE

Light from a huge August moon streamed through the window, throwing a path of brightness across the living room floor. On the mantel a pair of tall candles were lit, their flames illuminating a row of family photographs. Three generations of radiant brides and proud grooms stood in various poses, frozen when they were young and their futures stretched seamlessly and promisingly before them.

On the floor, nine-year-old Faith sat cross-legged opposite a ouija board from her brother. Each of them had their fingers resting lightly on the pointer that moved slowly and mysteriously over the board.

Her large dark eyes glistened with expectation and her vivid imagination raced. It was as if a door were about to be opened to a place she had never been before. The rest of her life stretched out in front of her, a blank waiting to be filled in. The possibilities were endless and she could barely contain her excitement. The man who would be her destiny was about to be revealed.

Except . . .

She frowned at her brother. "Stop *pushing* it, Larry. You're not supposed to force it. You're supposed to just let it happen."

"I'm not pushing it. You're pushing it."

"I am not. Just because you're three years older you think you're so smart and can get away with anything. *Lookit.* You just did it again."

"No, I didn't. Besides, this is dumb. We should be asking the board a good question like who's going to win the Series, not about who you're going to fall in love with. Who cares anyway?"

"You're pushing it," she said anxiously. "Stop it! *Maaa.* Larry's pushing it."

"Larry, don't push it." Their mother's automatic response drifted in from the next room.

"I'm not," Larry said stubbornly. "It's moving itself."

Faith gasped as the arrow began to move with more purpose toward a letter. It was working! "Wait. I have to write this down."

Larry groaned. "Once it starts working, you're not supposed to take your hands off it."

"Just one hand." She grabbed for a pencil and paper and started writing as the arrow moved from one letter to another. "Grandma says everybody has a soul mate. This way I'll know his name. The one I'm supposed to wait for. The one that'll wait for me."

Outside, the moon slipped behind a bank of clouds and the room darkened, but Faith barely noticed. She was too caught up in the letters as they were revealed one by one.

Larry's expression was skeptical. "Okay, but Faith, what if this guy lived a billion, trillion years ago? Like, what if he was a caveman and now he's dead?"

"Don't be stupid, Larry. Soul mates are our destiny. They live when we live."

"Yeah, but what if he doesn't live here in Pittsburgh? Like, what if he's a Vulcan like Spock?"

She copied down another letter. "Fate wouldn't make a mistake like that."

He wasn't about to let her off the hook that easily. "Okay, but Faith, what if he does live here and one day you pass him on the street? I mean, you just *pass* him without seeing him."

"That couldn't happen, Larry. I'd know. And you'll know too, 'cause you have a soul mate. We all do."

Larry stared at her for a moment, then looked down at the pointer. It had come to a halt. "Look."

Faith wrote down the final letter. Outside, the moon broke through the clouds and as it did a bright white beam of light pierced through the darkness to shine directly onto the name she had written.

"*Damon Bradley*," Faith said in an awed whisper. She looked up at her brother, spellbound. "My other half! My *soul mate*."

"Great," Larry said unimpressed. "Can I ask about the Series now?"

1977

There was something magical about the night, Faith thought, taking in the sights and sounds of the carnival around her. Something out of the ordinary. It was filled with secrets and possibilities and she wanted to discover and experience them all.

Above her, stars glittered in a night sky so clear, she was sure if she looked hard enough she would be able to see all the way to heaven. Colored lights hung in the trees and looped from booth to booth. The smell of popcorn and hot dogs saturated the air. The whimsical organlike sounds of a calliope competed with the thrilled screams of kids on the various rides. Wonderful horses painted in bright colors looked as if any second they would fly off the merry-go-round and take flight.

It was a night where anything could happen.

"You go first, go on. . . ."

Faith's attention snapped back to her group of friends and the booth in front of them. MADAME DIVINA'S FORTUNE-TELLING BOOTH.

"Cathy wants to know if she's gonna marry Alex," Leslie said with a big grin that exposed her brand-new set of braces.

"I do not," Cathy said with disdain, flipping her hair behind her shoulders. "He doesn't even have a brain."

"But he's got pretty eyes. That means your kids would have pretty eyes."

"I think you're all wrong," Faith said. "It's not about whether or not he has pretty eyes. It's whether or not he's your one true love." She turned to her best friend, who was studiously looking at the ground. "What do you think, Kate?"

"I don't know." Kate's delicate features were carefully schooled into an indifferent expression. "I guess I never really thought about it." Her long blond hair shifted across her back as she threw a quick glance up at the Ferris wheel.

"Look out below!"

The girls glanced up just in time to see Larry high above them in the Ferris wheel. Leaning over the safety bar, he was holding an enormous water balloon.

Faith planted her hands on her hips and yelled up at her brother. "Don't you dare, Larry! Don't you *dare*."

With a laugh, he sent the balloon torpedoing toward them. It hit the ground with an enormous *splat,* splashing them all with water.

Leslie and Cathy squealed with outrage.

"*Larry,*" Kate yelled at the top of her lungs. "I *hate* you!"

Faith shook her finger at him. "Stop that right now, Larry, or I'll tell Mom."

"*Next.*" The imperious summons came from inside Madame Divina's booth.

The girls fell silent and looked at each other.

Cathy shook her head. "*I'm* not going first."

Leslie glanced at Kate. "What about you?"

"What?" Kate asked, her attention held by the Ferris wheel as the ride began to slow down.

"I asked you if you wanted to go in first."

"I'll go," Faith said decisively, and ducked behind the curtain of glass beads and then the heavy rug that served as the booth's door.

But once inside, she stopped, unable to see anything. The room was dimly lit and the sounds of the carnival were muted, faraway. Gradually her eyes adjusted and she realized she had stepped into another world, a *mystical* world. Dark-colored material was bunched in corners and draped across the ceiling, giving the room a tentlike, exotic feeling. It even smelled different, she thought, noticing the smoke curling out of a brass incense burner.

Suddenly a match flared in the center of the room. Startled, Faith jumped. Then she saw Madame Divina sitting before a table, the match in her hand, her eyes half closed as if in deep concentration. Seemingly unaware of the flame burning closer and closer to her fingers, she set about with great ceremony to light a candle in front of her.

Faith was mesmerized. She had never in her life seen anyone like Madame Divina. She was big and imposing and she was wearing an even bigger and more imposing caftan. A row of unruly bright-red curls eluded a vivid purple scarf that was wound like a turban around her head. A myriad of bangle bracelets encircled one arm and her fingers were crowded with rings made of mysterious-looking stones. Large clusters of moons and stars were affixed at her ears, and string after string of colorful glass beads cascaded over her magnificent bosom.

Shivering with excitement, Faith wrapped her arms around her waist. How wonderful, how really *wonderful.* Madame Divina—who knew all and saw all—was about to reveal her future to her.

Suddenly the woman reached beneath the table and a large crystal ball in the center of the table was illuminated. Faith drew in an astonished breath.

"What secrets do you wish Madame Divina to reveal?"

Faith gestured vaguely. "Basic destiny stuff. But I don't want to hear anything bad, if that's okay."

There was a loud knock at the back of the booth and Faith started.

Madame Divina shrugged dismissively. "Spirits."

Faith's eyes grew big. "Really?"

Madame Divina waved her hand toward the chair opposite her. "Come. Sit down. We will start." She waited until Faith was seated, then closed her eyes and began to chant. "Oh, wise spirits, visit with us tonight and . . ."

"Pssssttt." Something banged against the back of the booth.

Without opening her eyes, Madame Divina hollered, *"Harry, I'm outta change.* Oh, wise spirits—"

The knocking became more persistent. "Dammit, Harry," she muttered. Clearly annoyed, she rose and lumbered toward the back of the booth. "What do you want?"

For a spirit, Harry was certainly persistent, Faith reflected nervously, watching her go. She looked back at the crystal ball. Surely it wouldn't hurt anything if she took just one little peek. She leaned forward and gazed into it. Nothing. She tried again from a different angle. Nothing. She sat back, somewhat disappointed. It must reveal its secrets only to Madame Divina, she decided.

Behind her the glass beads rustled and the rug was tugged aside. She turned to see Kate peering in. "What's your destiny?"

"Nothing so far. She had to go talk to a spirit."

"A spirit? What kind of spirit?"

"A spirit named Harry."

"Harry? That's a funny name for a—"

"Now we will proceed," Madame Divina said, returning.

"*Hey, Kate. Larry wants you.*" The call came from outside.

"*I do not,*" Larry yelled from somewhere close.

With a wide grin at Faith, Kate ducked back out.

Madame Divina sat down, closed her eyes, and began to finger the crystal ball. Completely entranced, Faith watched.

"Something is coming to me," Madame

Divina said softly. "I'm getting . . . a name. Yes, a name that's very important . . ."

Breathless with anticipation, Faith leaned forward. A faint breeze fluttered through the room and the candle flames flickered.

Madame Divina's face screwed up into an expression that showed the intense effort of the task at hand. "Da—David."

Faith let out a long, disappointed breath. "David?"

"No, no, wait . . . Damon."

Faith's heart skipped a beat. "Damon?" she whispered, awestruck.

"His name is . . ." Madame Divina's eyes popped open and she stared at Faith, her eyes glittering with startling intensity. "His name is *Damon Bradley*."

"Oh . . . my . . . God." Faith surged up from the chair. "I have to go."

Madame Divina's ringed fingers seized Faith's wrist, jerking her to a halt. Faith froze.

"Your destiny," Madame Divina said calmly, "is two dollars."

Faith pulled the money from her pocket and half threw it on the table, then turned to leave, but once again Madame Divina stopped her.

Still holding her wrist, the woman stood and pulled Faith toward her until her body was angled across the table and their faces were very close.

Madame Divina's eyes were now glittering so brightly, it was as if she had a fever. "The truth is, you make your own destiny. Understand? Don't wait for it to come to you. *You make your own.*"

Shocked, dazed, Faith nodded.

PRESENT DAY

IFaith stood before her junior high class, her glossy dark hair cut short and chic, her slim figure dressed every bit as hip and fashionable as her students. As she lectured, she wrote on the chalkboard.

DESTINO

". . . from the Latin destinare, meaning to have destination. To journey. To take a trip where the events are totally predetermined. Imagine that!" Excitedly she turned to her students. "The notion of an invincible necessity—a divine preordination, a—"

As the faces of her fourteen-year-old students registered confusion, she broke off her lecture and smiled. The only student who appeared to understand what she was talking about was Alicia, a serious-minded girl with hair down to her waist. She was fascinated by what Faith had said. Robert, the boy in the chair next to hers, appeared fascinated only with Alicia.

"Look." Faith lifted her hands in the air to demonstrate, determined that they all understand. "One hand, the other hand. Two separate hands, right? But put them together and what do they make?" She clasped her hands together and entwined her fingers.

"One," Alicia said.

Faith beamed at her. "Right. Plato tells us that we began as circles. And when we strived to be like gods, we were punished by a thunderbolt that struck us and cut us right down dead center in half."

She studied her students' reaction. Several of them recoiled at the idea, but others seemed to think it was cool. She continued. "We scattered to the ends of the earth, searching for our other half. And all Plato is saying is if we just stop . . . and follow our destiny, it will bring us to each other."

The bell rang, and commotion erupted as books closed, desks moved, and the kids bolted from their seats. She raised her voice. "Following through on this, read from your green book . . ." She pointed to the blackboard, where she had written WORDSWORTH, KEATS, AND SHELLEY.

"Bye, Miss Corbett."

"Thanks, Miss Corbett."

Slowly she erased the names of the poets, then the word *destino*, letter by letter. By the time the O was gone, the classroom was empty.

She took a seat at her desk, but instead of starting in on the stack of papers that needed to be graded, she contemplated the top drawer of the desk. Several moments passed before she slowly slid it open, pulled out a little black box, and flipped up the lid.

A diamond ring nestled in the black velvet interior of the box. A very *nice* diamond ring.

She slipped the ring on her finger and held up her hand. It was a beautiful ring, she thought objectively. Not too big, not too small. Just the right size, really. But it looked strange on her hand, foreign. Natural, she supposed, since she had never worn an engagement ring before. She could get used to it though. What woman couldn't get used to a diamond ring?

She folded her hands together as she had done for her class. Two separate hands put together to symbolically make one.

As a young girl, she had been enthralled with the idea that there was one special person chosen by destiny to be her soul mate. It had all seemed magical then. Possible. *Easy.*

But she was thirty now and things weren't always as easy as they had been then. She had learned that life could be very complicated and that the process of finding someone to spend the rest of your life with was much more complex than watching a ouija board pointer pick out a name.

Still, every weekend around the world countless couples married. Of course countless couples also divorced every day of the week. But she would never get a divorce. No, she had waited for years to marry so that she would be absolutely sure, and now here she was, on the brink of joining her life with someone else's to make one. And she was discovering that *brinks* could be scary.

She stared at her hands a moment longer before pulling them apart and replacing the ring in its box. She looked at her empty hand, then turned to gaze out the window.

"I understood what you were saying, Miss Corbett."

Starting at the sound of the young girl's voice, Faith turned and saw Alicia standing by her desk. "You did?"

Alicia nodded. "Yes."

Faith smiled. "Read *Love's Labor's Lost,*" she said gently. "There's a lot to it."

"Thanks, Miss Corbett, I will."

Faith placed a pizza on the coffee table in front of her two friends, then paused to light two candles. "What are you reading, Kate?"

Kate gazed over the rim of her glasses at her sister-in-law. "It's my sociology textbook. I've gone back to school. I'm taking a night class."

"Why, for goodness' sake?" Leslie asked, keeping an eye on the television. Her fire-engine-red hair was brighter than the flames on the candles and permed and teased to an incredible volume. "And when do you see yourself having time to study?"

"The kids are in school now. Even with everything I have to do I think I can find some time, even if maybe the floors don't get scrubbed one week or the laundry goes an extra day. I think it's going to be good for me. Sociology is something I've always been interested in and Larry is always so busy. . . ."

Leslie reached over and patted Kate on the knee. "I didn't mean to sound negative. I think it's a wonderful idea."

"Thanks."

Leslie nodded, then looked back at the television screen and the flickering images of *The Arthur Godfrey Show.* "Do you have any idea what this is we're watching?"

Faith smiled. "It's a PBS documentary about TV's golden age and since none of us is watching it, why don't you turn it down so we can talk."

Leslie promptly reached for the remote control and Faith poured their Coke into wineglasses.

Kate put the book aside, shoved her glasses on top of her head, and reached for a glass. "Okay, Faith, what's this all about? I know you. Something's special about you tonight. You've got that look."

Leslie scrutinized her friend. "Kate's right, Faith. "What's up?"

Faith twined her fingers together, then, realizing what she had done, pulled her hands apart and slipped them into her pockets. But feeling the ring in her right pocket, she withdrew her hands and let them hang by her sides. Lord, why was this so hard?

"He proposed."

Leslie's mouth fell open."

"No!" Kate's hand jerked, sending Coke splashing over the rim of the wineglass onto her hand. As she sat the glass on the end table, she made a quick study of her best friend. "And you're happy?"

Faith tilted her head to one side and smiled faintly.

"*Yes!* She's happy!" Kate jumped up off the sofa, sidestepped the coffee table, and enveloped Faith in a big hug. "That's great!"

Leslie's smile filled her whole face as she hurried over to Faith to be next in line for a hug. "I'm so happy for you. Did he get down on his knees?"

Faith tried to imagine a situation that might get Dwayne on his knees and decided that only the act of lining up a golf shot would do it. And there hadn't been a golf ball or a putting green in sight when he had proposed. "Well . . ."

"That's okay if he didn't," Kate said quickly. "Dwayne's a practical man who understands how bad kneeling can be for the knees. So, when's the date?"

"The date?"

Kate's expression was concerned. "You did set a date, didn't you?"

"Well, no, not—I don't think we should rush into anything."

"Rush into anything?" Leslie looked shocked. "Faith, you've been seeing him for—"

"Where's the ring?" Kate interrupted, her tone suspicious. "Did you say yes?"

Slowly Faith reached into her pocket and pulled the ring from her pocket.

Kate's hand flew to her eyes. "I'm blind! I'm blind!"

"Where are my sunglasses?" Leslie pulled Faith's hand closer. "What a *rock*. I hate you. I want one. Lord, it's gorgeous, Faith."

Kate crossed her arms. "So tell us again why it isn't on your finger?"

"I asked him to give me one day to think about it, okay? I am entitled to give myself one day to think about the rest of my life. I'm never going to divorce. So I'll think about it. Okay?" She looked from Kate to Leslie. They wore identical expressions of disappointment. "I'm just telling you what I told him. I needed some mental space so I could reflect and then say yes."

Leslie sighed.

Kate frowned.

"Oh, for God's sake, I told my parents I'm engaged."

Leslie clapped her hands together. *"Yeah!"*

Kate threw her arms around her again for a quick hug. "That's great. I really am so happy for you. Dwayne's quite a catch. He's a sane, nonsmoking heterosexual male and—"

Leslie took up the list. "He's intelligent—"

"Athletic—"

"He has a good sense of humor—"

"He has no sense of humor," Faith interjected wryly.

Kate spread out her arms. "No more struggling on a teacher's salary. He's a *doctor*, for crying out loud. He saves lives!"

"He's a foot doctor."

Kate shrugged. "He saves feet."

Leslie nodded in emphatic agreement and Kate reached for a nearby photograph of Dwayne. Leslie pointed to the picture. "Plus, he's tall. Your kids'll be tall."

Faith grabbed the photo out of Kate's hands and put it back on the table. Before

Dwayne had given her a picture of himself, she had always thought it highly egotistical to give a person a picture of oneself unless that person were a parent or a grandparent. Or unless the picture had been asked for. Which it hadn't. But she did love the picture. After all, it was of the man she was going to marry.

"Dwayne's a very nice man. And you two don't have to list his good points to me. He's as good as gold. And"—she eyed her pizza critically—"I need some pepper." She vanished into the kitchen.

Kate plopped back onto the sofa and helped herself to a slice of the pizza. "Faith, don't wait," she called with her mouth half full. "You wait and you'll wind up with nothing."

"I don't exactly consider my life nothing," she said, returning to the room with the pepper.

Kate swallowed her mouthful. "All I'm saying is he's a doctor, don't let him get away. Remember that junior high principal, he wanted to marry you. Kids loved him, Leslie and I loved him."

Faith dropped down into a chair with a frown.

Leslie nodded. "Del Russo. He was nuts

about you. And what about that fitness freak?"

"Right," Kate said. "Rick Miller with that flat, tight, rippled stomach. Remember that stomach? He was awesome."

Faith contemplated her pepper-ladened slice of pizza. "Yeah, he was and so was Del Russo. And they each deserve all the happiness in the world." She took a bite. "I think I put too much pepper on this."

"What exactly is it you think you're waiting for?" Kate asked, perplexed.

"I'm not waiting."

"You have been. And I don't understand it. You want children and a family, which is why I—"

"I'm *not* waiting."

"Okay, good, then let's see that ring on your finger."

She slipped it on and wiggled her fingers at her friends. "Happy now?"

Kate grinned. "It's a start. Now we can discuss bridesmaid dresses."

Instantly on guard, Leslie held up a hand. "Nothing pink. Promise me, Faith. I look *terrible* in pink."

"I agree," Kate said. "And nothing salmon either. Remember Cathy's bridesmaid dresses? I can describe the color only as *fervently* salmon. I spent the entire reception in morbid fear that someone would slap garlic and butter on me and try to put me on a cracker."

Faith groaned. She didn't have a clue as to what color she'd like to have for her bridesmaid dresses, but she supposed she had better start thinking about that, along with some of the other decisions she was going to be faced with in the coming weeks.

The telephone rang. Thankful for the distraction, Faith reached for the portable phone.

"Hello?" Her solemn expression dissolved to a big smile. "Hi, Larry. Yeah, she's here. ld on." She held out the phone to Kate. "It's big brother for you."

Kate stared at the phone.

It's not a snake," Faith said playfully. your husband."

ight." She took the phone. "Hello."

ate, you're still there? I thought you'd your way home by now."

t the sound of his voice used to thrill te remembered, but now it made her nd more than a little sad. She imag- standing by his desk, wearing jeans and the T-shirt that had LARRY'S ROOFING written on it. And she remembered that he hadn't kissed her good-bye that morning. "Well, I'm not. I'm here with your sister and Leslie." She paused. "What is it? You miss me?"

"Yeah. Sure. Honey, did you forget what night it is? The guys are coming over for poker tonight. I mean, what are we gonna eat?"

"I'm a woman, not a menu. You want food, go to a deli."

"But I'm still at work. The guys will be there and there won't be anything to eat."

"Well, why don't you all go to the diner?" She saw Faith and Leslie exchange a glance, then become instantly absorbed in what was on television.

"But what about the kids?" Larry asked. "Aren't you going to make something for them to eat?"

"The kids are at Gus's birthday party." Her hand tightened on the receiver. "I told you a week ago, but you never listen."

"I listen, but it's my poker night."

"Right, *yours*. Not mine. Your poker night is not my responsibility." Larry mumbled something. The words were indistinguishable but the meaning wasn't. "Oh, *yeah*, Larry? Well, you can just fend for yourself. I'm not cooking for you." She punched the disconnect button and barely refrained from throwing the phone across the room.

On television a man appeared, singing "Some Enchanted Evening." Faith picked up the remote control and turned up the volume. "It's Ezio Pinza."

"Ezio who?" Leslie asked.

"He was in *South Pacific* on Broadway with Mary Martin. Oh, why did they stop writing romantic songs like this?"

Kate stood up and grabbed her sweater and purse. "I should go."

"No, wait. You gotta watch this." She slipped out of the chair and onto the sofa in the place vacated by Kate so that she could see the screen better. "Listen to those lyrics. Don't you just love it?"

Kate threw an annoyed look at the TV. "The shrinks on *Donahue* say those love songs are just a cruel hoax that feed people's fantasies. Romance on a daily basis? Nobody has that."

"But somebody wrote those songs. They came out of somebody's experience."

Kate stared at the screen. "No, Faith. They came out of somebody's imagination."

On the television screen Ezio Pinza sang, "Some enchanted evening . . ."

Kate slung her purse over her shoulder and sighed longingly.

Leslie's eyes misted at the emotions being sung so beautifully.

Faith listened, rapt.

"Some enchanted evening . . ." Faith sang beneath her breath as she slipped her nightgown over her head. She didn't want to think that romance and true love were a cruel hoax. In fact she couldn't. Surely sometime, somewhere, two people had looked at each other across a crowded room and known instantly that they were looking at their one true love. Of course, it hadn't happened like that for her and Dwayne.

She walked into the bathroom and reached for the bar of soap, remembering how they had met on a blind date. He had been early and she had dressed too casually for the ultra-chic restaurant he had taken her to. She had spent the night listening to the intricacies and complexities of caring for the feet and gone home glassy-eyed. But it had gotten

27

better after that. And just because nothing out of a love song had ever happened to the two of them didn't mean that he wasn't her destiny. He had given her a ring, hadn't he?

The *ring*. She glanced down at it. Soap film could diminish the sparkle, she reflected, and Dwayne would get upset if that happened. He was very proud of the sparkle. She took it off and laid it at the edge of the sink, then began to lather her face just as the phone rang. She decided to let the machine get it.

"Hi, honey. It's Mom."

Faith smiled faintly, listening with one ear.

"I called the bakery and made the appointment for us. And I've started the guest list. Oh, and Uncle Jack says he can get us a deal on the catering."

Faith's smile faded. She knew from years of watching her friends that planning a wedding could be the equivalent of planning a war. She didn't look forward to it starting.

"I'm so happy for you, sweetie. Here's Dad. Love you."

Her eyes narrowed as she noticed something in the mirror. She leaned closer and saw a single glistening gray hair. Good grief, had the thought of the wedding plans already begun to take its toll?

But it was just *one* gray hair. She could pull it and no one would ever know. She lifted her hand toward it, but then after a moment's thought slowly let her hand drop again. *No.* She'd leave it. Gray hair was a sign of maturity and advanced knowledge and in the coming months she was going to need plenty of both. Lord, that was a foreboding thought.

"Hey, kid, it's Dad. A *doctor.* Wait until my sister hears about this. Your grandma always said you were going to marry a special man. Congratulations, sweetheart!"

"Thanks, Dad," she said softly, still staring at herself in the mirror. She was tired, that was all. As soon as she and her mom started planning the wedding, she would get excited.

The machine clicked off, and with a sigh she left the bathroom, climbed into bed, and turned out the light. Snuggling down beneath the covers, she closed her eyes.

The *ring.*

Her eyes flew open. How could she have forgotten her ring? It wasn't just another piece of jewelry. It was a symbol of Dwayne's love for her, and by her accepting it, a symbol of her love for him. . . .

Guiltily she switched the light back on, slid out of bed, and made her way into the bathroom.

She slipped the ring on her finger, then looked at herself in the mirror. Yeah, she was tired, that was all.

A little bride and groom, their porcelain faces frozen in perpetual smiles, stood atop a massive wedding cake, rotating endlessly to "We've Only Just Begun." The song was coming out of speakers, one suspended from each corner of the well-lit bakery. Easy targets, Faith thought, eyeing them with speculation. If she had a gun, she'd shoot the speakers and put the little wedding pair out of their misery. Not to mention herself.

She and her mother had been in the bakery less than half an hour, but it felt like days to her. Not only was the song getting on her nerves, but developing a blood sugar problem was a real concern. The air smelled like sugar and was no doubt saturated with calories, cholesterol, and fat. Inhaling could definitely be dangerous.

"Okay, we're settling for the five-tier with the marzipan, without the almonds."

Faith turned her attention back to the woman behind the counter who had just spoken. She had a pad and pen in her hand and an apron circled her slender waist. She couldn't be eating what she sold, Faith concluded. Perhaps she knew something they didn't.

The woman went on. "Now, do you want one of those working fountains between the bottom layer and the top four layers of the cake? We can color-coordinate the water to match any bridesmaid dress. All I need is a swatch of material."

Faith blinked. "You're kidding, right?"

Clearly excited, her mother put her arm around her and gave her a squeeze. "Three weeks and counting, Faith. Your wedding will be such a beautiful day."

"I hope so, Mom." She turned and looked outside to see rain slashing against the big picture window in the front of the bakery.

But inside all was well. Karen Carpenter kept insisting, "We've only just begun . . ."

And the little bride and groom continued to rotate.

The heavy battering of rain had eased to a steady downpour by evening, creating little miniature lakes throughout Pittsburgh and making the streets hazardous to negotiate. But inside Dwayne's apartment the engagement party was in full swing.

Guests circulated throughout the upscale two-story town house that commanded a magnificent view of the city. The endless expanse of white carpet was broken by islands of black leather couches and chairs and custom-designed marble tables, with touches of red here and there to add visual interest. At least that's what Dwayne's decorator had said, Faith remembered.

The equally white walls were dolloped with modern art so startlingly abstract, she couldn't help but wonder how her beloved prints would fit in, especially the one of the rainbow slicing through a cloudy sky to arc over a sienna-colored cliff.

High-tech stereo equipment played music that to her ears sounded the way vanilla ice cream tasted. It was the kind of music you heard without realizing you were hearing it. But at least it wasn't "We've Only Just Begun."

"Oh, well, she reflected philosophically. Love conquered all, and she and Dwayne would work everything out . . . somehow.

And this was her engagement party, a happy moment she had looked forward to practically her whole life. And the man she loved was by her side, holding her hand out so that the people around them could admire the ring he had bought her. What more could she want?

"Beautiful, Faith," someone said.

"Thank you." What was wrong with her? She had the strangest feeling that she could leave her hand where it was, there in the center of the group so that the ring could continue to be admired, walk away, and no one would notice she was missing.

In one corner a massive espresso machine hissed. In another a champagne cork popped. The rain and music continued.

Someone else in the group spoke up. "Must've been at least five grand . . ."

Beside her, Dwayne, tall, handsome, and distinguished in his glasses, smiled proudly. "I really enjoyed researching this diamond."

He moved Faith's hand so that the light caught in the stone, and she gave a small prayer of thanks that she had been diligent in protecting the ring from soap scum.

"I learned a great deal about gemstones." He winked at the group to alert them to his upcoming wit. "It's amazing all the variations you can find of pure carbon crystallized in regular octahedrons." He slid his arm around her. "But, seriously, here's my gemstone. Right here."

Faith smiled and felt a vague pain near her temple. Dwayne was such a nice man. She was really so lucky.

He patted her on her shoulder and leaned down to give her a tender peck on her cheek.

The vague ache turned into a sharp pain. Funny, she never got headaches. But now even her smile hurt. And she felt extremely awkward with everyone in the group looking at her expectantly, like a trophy Dwayne was showing off. And since it was Dwayne, that would make her a *golf* trophy.

"Excuse me," she murmured, and moved away, taking her hand with her. But she hadn't gotten three feet when her mother grabbed her and dragged her over to meet two very large women standing beneath a new abstract Dwayne had just acquired, its main colors yellow and orange, much like the hue of the blotchy skin of one of the women.

"Faith, I'd like you to meet Frances Steinmetz and Jane Merriweather. They're Dwayne's aunts from Philadelphia on his mother's side."

Faith summoned her smile once again. "How do you do. It's very nice to meet you. Thank you for coming tonight."

The women beamed at her in unison. Jane, the one with the blotchy skin, spoke up first. "Dwayne is our favorite nephew and we are simply thrilled with his engagement."

Frances nodded knowingly. "You are one very lucky young woman to have caught our Dwayne."

"I was just thinking that very thing," she said sweetly, and wondered if blotchy skin and weight problems ran in Dwayne's family. She glanced around the room for Kate.

Out on the covered terrace, Kate looked at her husband in disgust. "Not only is it tacky, it's exploitation."

"It's not exploitation. These people wanna sell and I wanna buy." He turned to the woman standing with them to plead his case. "How are golf clubs exploitation? She takes one night class and suddenly she's a so-cialist."

"Sociologist. And it's my major." Kate held up her hand and ticked off several points on her fingers. "Pawnshops are just like prosti-tutes, farm auctions, and miners. They're all for sale, but none of them would be if they weren't desperate for the money. You're tak-ing advantage of the disadvantaged."

"We're all desperate for the money, doll. That's what made this country great." He turned again to the woman standing with them. "Back me up on this, Josie. Am I right?"

Kate forestalled anything Josie might have said. "Don't call me doll, Larry. It's de-grading."

With a polite, embarrassed murmur Josie slipped away.

"You used to like it when I called you doll," Larry said tensely.

"You said it differently then." She hugged herself and gazed unhappily at the rain. There had been real feeling in the way he used to call her doll, she remembered. He used to say it as if she were something he cherished. Now he sounded patronizing.

Larry threw up his hands, a gesture she

knew meant he thought she was being unreasonable. She and Larry couldn't talk anymore, and she was scared. Her marriage was coming apart right before her eyes and she didn't know how to save it. Or even if she wanted to.

Happily unaware of any of the undercurrents running between the two, Leslie joined them. "God, I hope it doesn't rain on Faith's wedding day. But then, don't they say that it means good luck or something like that?"

"That's just something they say to brides to make them feel better," Kate said. It had rained on her wedding day, she remembered.

The three of them turned and gazed through the open door into the party at Faith.

Dwayne's mother handed Faith a large, heavy white box. "Here, darling. This is for you."

Faith lifted off the top to reveal a wedding gown that had been in fashion thirty or thirty-five years ago. She glanced uncertainly at Dwayne's mother. "Is this yours?"

"I wore it, my daughter wore it, and I want you to have the same joy. And I must say I was thrilled when Dwayne said you would wear it."

Faith's smile felt frozen. Now she knew

how the little bride and groom on top of the cake felt. "Dwayne said that?" She glanced across the room at her fiancé, who was leaning with one hand against the large stone sculpture of a foot that was his pride and joy, talking with a group of his college buddies. As she watched she saw him smile from ear to ear, obviously relishing the story he was telling.

Dwayne laughed, shaking his head. "And then my nurse said, 'Gee, Dr. Johnson, you really put your foot in your mouth that time.'" His friends groaned and he laughed again. "She's priceless, that nurse of mine." Glancing across the room, he saw Faith waving to him. "I'll be right back, guys. Have some more champagne." He crossed to her side. "Hi, honey. Having fun?"

"Fun? Yes. May I see you a moment?" She headed for the nearest unoccupied corner, lugging the box with her. Once they reached relative privacy, she handed the burden of the box over to him.

"You told your mother I would wear this dress? How *could* you?"

"Faith, it would mean so much to her."

Her head now felt as if a jackhammer were getting up close and personal with it. "It means a lot to me too, Dwayne. It's my wedding too. And this dress is not what I want to wear. I always pictured—"

"She's not a young woman, darling. We can find it in our hearts to humor her, can't we? Just think about it, okay?"

"But it's just . . ."

"Hey, look, your father wants to take our picture. Wait a second." He set the box on a nearby table, then turned to her. "You're not going to leave your hair like that, are you?"

She lifted her hand to her hair, unsure what the problem was or what she should do about it.

Dwayne brushed her hand aside. "Let me." He smoothed an errant strand of glossy brown hair that had fallen onto her forehead back into place so that it lay neatly against her head. "There. Now you're perfect." He shifted positions, put his arm around her, and pulled her against his side. *"Smile."*

Thunder boomed overhead and Faith flinched. In front of her a flash popped and everything went blindingly white.

With her arms behind her back, Faith strained and contorted to fasten the seem ingly endless string of tiny satin buttons that ran from hip to neckline of her mother-in-law-to-be's wedding dress. And she was losing the battle, she thought grimly. Buttoning this dress could take a lifetime. When would she have time to have kids, much less raise them?

"Don't look yet," she said a bit breathlessly.

"Tell me when," Kate said from the next room. "Sorry I'm late by the way. The kids are going up to the lake with my mom and dad for Labor Day weekend. I had to get everything ready. Dwayne's not coming over, is he?"

"No, he had an emergency matrixectomy. Okay, you can look."

Kate walked into the room and Faith twirled so that she could get the full effect of the wedding gown.

"Oh, Faith, look at you. God, in one week you will be a married woman."

"Ten days." She stared at herself in her living room mirror. "It's sort of romantic, I guess. Wearing the gown of the woman who bore your husband. I mean, maybe my daughter will wear it someday too."

If the box had been heavy, the dress was even heavier. And tight. And *oppressive*. She couldn't seem to breathe, and at the same time she was breathing too much, in danger of hyperventilating. In danger of suffocating. "Kate, would you open a window, please?"

"Sure." She crossed to the nearest window and raised it.

Faith smoothed her hand down over the skirt. The skirt and the petticoats were made up of lace and net, miles and miles of it. "It was sweet of her, wasn't it?"

"Yeah, I guess," Kate said, moving back to Faith. She adjusted the shoulders on the gown, then turned her attention to the long row of buttons. "You missed a few. Breathe in."

"I'm not surprised. This dress obviously cornered the world market on buttons when it was made." She held her breath while Kate finished fastening the dress. "It's not quite like it is in the movies, is it?"

Kate finished and handed her a long white glove. "That's the problem. When you're a kid, everyone conspires to tell you that. Mothers, fathers, teachers, priests. Right? Dreams come true, the good guys win, people live happily ever after—all that crap." She bent her head to help Faith on with the glove.

"Wait a minute. The fingers of this glove

are too small to fit over the ring." She slipped the ring off and held it out. "Would you go put this in the top drawer of my dresser, please?"

"Sure." Kate disappeared into the bedroom. When she came back, she took up the conversation where she had left off. "Anyway, one day you wake up and realize you've been had."

"But what about dreams? And magic and romance? Things like flowers and poetry and unforgettable moments—those are the important things. What would the world be like without them?" She glanced at her friend and saw that she had tears in her eyes. "Kate, what's the matter?"

"I dunno," Kate said shakily, staring up at the ceiling. "Listen, there's something I want to talk to you about."

Instantly concerned she turned to her. "What is it?"

"I think—"

The phone rang.

"Don't move. Dwayne's having his calls forwarded. I have to answer that, but I'll be right back."

Her movements were awkward as she made her way into the kitchen. Who would have thought lace and net could be so heavy?

Of course there was about an *ocean* of lace and net along with those damned buttons. She lifted the receiver. "Hello?"

"Dr. Dwayne Johnson? I'm trying to reach Dr. Johnson."

Faith could barely hear, there was so much background noise coming from the other end of the line. "No, he's not in at the moment. He's doing an emergency matrixectomy. Can I take a message?"

"Who's this?"

"This is Faith, his fiancée. Who's this?"

"Oh, hi. I'm an old high school buddy of Dwayne's. Congratulations on your wedding. I'll be in Europe, so I'll miss your big day."

"Oh, sorry to hear that." Faith glanced toward the living room, wondering what Kate wanted to tell her. "What's your name?"

"My name's . . ." His voice was drowned out by noise.

"I can hardly hear you. Could you spell it?" She grabbed a pad and pen and began writing. Letter by letter she wrote, and for the second time in her life she spelled out the name *Damon Bradley.*

She stared at the name, dumbstruck. "Damon Bradley . . ." The phone slipped from her hand and clattered to the floor.

Kate walked in. "What? Why'd you drop the phone?"

"Right," came the man's faint voice from the receiver on the floor. "Thanks a lot. And congrats. It's not easy finding love these days."

Kate looked at her friend. "Who is it?"

Faith grabbed up the phone. "Damon Bradley? Where are you?"

Kate's eyes widened and her mouth formed "Damon Bradley" as she tried to place the name. It sounded so familiar to her. . . .

"I'm at the airport. Why?"

Kate snapped her fingers. "Damon Bradley? Isn't that the guy?"

"Shhh." Faith waved her away. "At the airport?"

"I'm on my way to Venice. And my trip's extended, so—"

"Is it that guy?" Kate asked, whispering.

"Oh, Venice?" Faith tried to think fast. For most of her life she had waited for Damon Bradley, and now here he was on the other end of the phone, about to leave the country. And she was about to get married. There had to be some significance to the call and some way—

"I love *Venice*. I've never seen it in person, but they say it's the pearl of the Adriatic."

"Huh? Uh, yeah. I gotta run. Maybe someday we can all get together."

She heard a click, then a dial tone. "But wait! Hello? Hello? Oh, God, he hung up!" She stood there, clinging desperately to the receiver.

"What is going on?"

She hung up the phone and whirled toward Kate, her eyes wide with excitement. "My God, Kate, he's *here*. In *Pittsburgh*. At the *airport*. Get me out of this dress!"

"There's a million buttons!"

"Forget it, you're right. Call a cab."

"For where?"

"The airport! I'm going downstairs." In an attempt to camouflage the dress, she grabbed her coat and whipped it on, but a good two feet of lace and net billowed out from beneath the coat's hem.

"*Wait!* Faith!" Kate realized she was staring at an empty apartment because Faith was gone. She grabbed the phone and began dialing, all the while mumbling to herself. "Damon Bradley at the Pittsburgh airport?" The cab company answered and she quickly gave them the address.

The weight of the wedding dress dragged at Faith as she took the stairs down to the ground floor of the apartment building three at a time, the back hem of the dress trailing several steps behind her. She pushed the front door open and raced out onto the street. There were no cabs in sight. She glanced at her watch. *Please let him be there when I get there.*

"It's a coincidence, Faith," Kate called, leaning out of the second-story-apartment window.

She turned and looked up at her friend. "This is *not* a coincidence. When you and I come home with the same pair of shoes, that's a coincidence! Kate, I know you think I'm crazy, but I just want to get a look at him, that's all."

She spotted her cab down the street and gave a two-fingered whistle that would have made a longshoreman proud. She waved to Kate, then, when the cab drew to the curb, jumped in. "The airport."

The cabdriver, a bald-headed, unflappable man old enough to be her father, pulled out into the flow of traffic.

She leaned forward. "Please go faster. *Please.*"

"Departures or arrivals?" he asked calmly.

"Departures. International."

The driver looked over his shoulder at her. "You sure travel light, lady."

3

The cab squealed around the corner and pulled to a stop outside the terminal. Faith thrust a handful of bills at the driver and jumped out. Then, after getting directions at a ticket counter inside the terminal, she took off running down the long corridor.

What was she doing?

Larry had been on the track team in high school. She, on the other hand, had always hated running. But she was possessed by the spirit of the little girl who had played with a Ouija board and believed in the possibilities of the unknown and who had gazed wide-eyed at Madame Divina as the woman magically told her the very same name of the man who was supposed to be her destiny. That *couldn't* be a coincidence. It just couldn't be. But if it were, it was time she found out now, *before* she married Dwayne.

Reaching the escalators, she skidded to a stop. Both of the escalators were going the wrong way and she couldn't see any stairs. Gathering up a handful of the long, white skirt and petticoats, she sprinted up the down escalator. Unfortunately the escalator was barely wide enough for two people, and in the wedding dress she was almost the width of two people. By the time she reached the top of the escalator she had lost count of the startled faces she had passed and the times she had murmured, "Excuse me."

In Corridor C she jumped on the people mover, but it was so crowded she couldn't move. She vaulted over the side, and for the first time in her life actually wished she *had* taken track. Despite her twice-weekly aerobics class, she was in no shape for what had basically turned into a track and field event.

Running at full tilt, she threaded her way through an arriving basketball team and finally slid to a stop at TWA Gate 34 just as the attendant, a man smartly buttoned into a navy blue uniform, closed the jetway door.

Her life was being taken over by buttons, she thought inconsequentially.

"Flight 417," she said breathlessly. "Is it still here?"

The man surveyed the wedding dress with suspicion. "The flight's closed. We do ask that you be here an hour in advance. Your boarding pass, please?"

"I—I must've misplaced it." Glancing out the window, she saw that mechanics were preparing to detach the jetway from the plane.

"I'm sorry, but without a boarding pass we cannot let you on the plane."

She started digging through her purse and at the same time inching her way past the rope used to block people. The attendant followed and grabbed her arm.

Her eyes moistened with tears as she looked up at him. "I'm sure I've got it here someplace. . . ."

This can't be happening, she thought wildly. She couldn't be this close to Damon Bradley and not be able to see him. As a teenager she had spent hours daydreaming about Damon Bradley. She had wondered where he was, what he was doing, what he was like, and most important, she had wondered if he was dreaming about her as she was about him. And she had filled pages and pages of notebook paper with the names *Mrs. Damon Bradley* and *Faith Bradley*.

And now he was so close. . . .

"Great. Because as I said, until you find the boarding pass, we can't let you on the plane."

"Okay," she said, panic setting in. "You're right. I don't have a boarding pass, but I have to give a man on the plane a very important message. So couldn't you open the door for just a second and let me in?" Oh, God, the jetway was about to be removed. She tried to push past him.

"We have very strict rules." He grabbed her arm and got her glove. "They are for your own safety." He tried to pull her back and her white glove began to slip off.

"It's a real emergency. Please, please . . . just this once."

The attendant struggled with her and her glove slipped down to her wrist.

"But don't you understand? You could affect my *life!*"

"Right, uh, just a moment." Holding her with one hand, he used his other to pick up his phone.

Faith glanced out the window to see the plane start to taxi away from the gate.

"Yeah, this is Bill over at TWA." He lowered his voice. "We've got a two three seven on our hands here. Uh-huh. Yeah. Thanks." He hung up and with his best plastic, humoring-a-crazy-person smile, said, "It'll be just a moment." In the distance he saw a security guard approaching and he waved to him.

Faith broke away from the attendant and hurried over to the window. She watched as the plane slowly taxied away into the darkness. She pressed her hand to the window as if doing so would allow her to reach out and touch Damon Bradley. He was about to leave her life before he had ever entered it, and she felt incredibly sad. The guard stopped behind her.

She glanced over her shoulder at him, then looked back at the plane. "The man I was supposed to marry is on that plane."

She and the guard watched until the plane disappeared from view. And they continued to stand there until the plane lifted off into the night.

With a white-gloved hand Faith picked up her cup of coffee and finished it, then sat slumped at the little table inside one of the airport bars, staring at nothing in particular. She barely noticed when her coat slipped from her shoulders. She should probably go home, she thought, but she had expended all her energy in the chase.

She caught the bartender's eye and motioned for a refill.

The bartender picked up the coffeepot and down at the end of the bar a man remarked, "Crazy world, huh? Nobody wants to get married in a church anymore."

With a shrug, the bartender walked over and poured her another cup. "You okay?"

No, she thought, she wasn't. She was wearing a wedding dress she'd probably never be able to get off, sitting in an airport bar while the man who was supposed to be her soul mate was at this moment winging his way to Venice. "I'm fine."

He motioned toward the departure screen. She glanced up at it but it looked blurry to her. She rubbed at her eyes. God, was she going blind too?

"Are you in the right area for your flight?" he asked. "Do you know how much time you have?"

"I'm not going any"—a sudden light flickered to life in her eyes—"where. . . ."

Standing on tiptoe, Faith leaned over the reservation agent's desk, studying the screen with her. After looking at the screen for the past five minutes, she almost understood what she was seeing.

"What about that one?" she said, pointing.

The reservation agent pushed several buttons, then studied the results. "Yeah, yeah, this is good. You connect at JFK to Flight 206 nonstop to Rome—wait a minute, it's not good. You have to change in Italy to a domestic terminal. Jeez, you'll only have forty minutes. You'll be exhausted."

"That's okay. What time would I be in Venice?"

"Kate, I'm doing it. . . ." Faith was stuffed into a phone booth, the wedding dress frothing and bubbling up around her like sea foam.

Was it possible, she wondered, to drown in sea foam made of lace? Eyeing the lace suspiciously, she decided that with this dress anything was possible.

She swatted at a particularly menacing poof. "Kate, you can't stop me. If I allow myself to leave this airport, I'll never go through with it. And if I don't, I'll regret it for the rest of my life. This is my last chance to find Damon Bradley. It's Labor Day weekend. I don't have a class till Wednesday. . . . *Thank you!* My passport's in the top left drawer of my desk, I need something light to wear, I don't care what, but don't forget my hair dryer. . . . You've got to hurry"—she glanced at her watch—"the plane leaves in an hour and twelve minutes."

The dress swishing around her, Faith paced back and forth in front of the information booth, alternately watching the clock and desperately looking for Kate. She had only twelve minutes left. . . .

She would have gotten on the plane in a heartbeat without a change of clothes—she could always buy what she needed in Venice—but her chances of getting on the plane without a passport were slim to none. She hadn't failed to notice that she wasn't exactly batting a thousand with airline attendants this evening.

Suddenly she saw Kate and Leslie rushing toward her, their arms loaded down with suitcases.

"Where have you been? I have *twelve* minutes."

Kate waved an airline ticket. "Buying my ticket. I'm coming with you."

"Are you *crazy?*"

Kate stopped before her. "No, *you're* crazy. Someone has to be with you before you do something really stupid that you'll regret."

"Okay, then, it's Gate 93. *Andiamo.*"

Faith led the way, racing up the same down escalator she had raced up over an hour earlier. Kate and Leslie dodged and ducked around people and their baggage, keeping pace a step behind her.

"I've got your jeans," Kate said, "and I've got that great red dress, the one you've never had the guts to wear. I gave you one pair of heels, your Reeboks—"

Leslie juggled a suitcase and a yearbook. "We stopped at the library. I found his yearbook. God, I wish I had a passport—God, I wish I were coming."

Faith's head whipped around. "Damon Bradley's yearbook?"

"Your *fiancé's* yearbook, which is also Damon Bradley's."

Faith bumped into someone. "Excuse me.

Have you found him?" She stepped on someone's heels. "Excuse me."

"Not yet." Leslie was flipping through the yearbook as she ran.

"I've got your hair dryer," Kate said, "but I think you need a special adapter so don't just plug it in, it might blow up on you. Why are we doing this?"

They jammed onto the people mover.

"What if Dwayne and I aren't really meant to be? Is it fair for me to waste his life?"

"She's right," Leslie said. "What if Damon Bradley's really her soul mate?"

At the security check area Kate threw her bag on the security belt, flashed her boarding card, and rushed through the metal detector. On the other side, she called, "Leslie, he's *not* her soul mate. She's never even met this man. She's spent her whole life waiting for somebody with his name—this name she got from a Parker Brothers game when she was just a kid."

Leslie continued to flip through the yearbook.

"You forgot about the fortune-teller," Faith said, racing through the metal detector. "She—"

The metal detector erupted with a loud, rude electronic beep.

"He's got to be here somewhere," Leslie said, continuing to look through the yearbook.

Faith hurried over to the security guard and hurled her house keys in the tray, then once again rushed through the detector.

Beep.

"Oh, my God. The plane will leave—"

"Your watch," the guard said.

She pushed her watch off her arm, put it into the tray, and rushed through again.

Beep.

Kate watched anxiously. "What have you got in there, Faith?"

"Open your coat," the guard ordered.

She jerked the edges of her coat apart. The guard glanced at the wedding dress, exchanged a look with another guard, then passed his hand scanner over the dress. The dress sent the scanner into an electronic fit.

"Those damned buttons," Faith murmured.

"Buttons?"

"Satin-covered metal buttons. About a kajillion of them down the back."

"Don't forget the stays," Kate called.

The guard looked at Faith curiously. "Are you coming or going to the wedding?"

"Neither."

"None of your business!" Kate yelled. "Let's go, Faith!"

The guard motioned her to go on. Kate and Faith turned and waved at Leslie, who was still frantically flipping through the yearbook, then grabbed up their bags and began to run toward the boarding gate.

Kate glanced over at Faith. "Are we just going to fly to Italy and comb the streets?

"He was on his way to Venice, right? While I was waiting for you I called six hotels in the city and found out where he's staying and made a reservation."

"So we can see him tomorrow and we're home the next day."

"Exactly."

By the time they reached the gate they were nearly out of breath. They passed the boarding passes to the attendant and started to the jetway. But a hand grabbed Faith's shoulder. Panic-stricken, she turned to the security guard.

"What?"

He handed her a contact lens case. "Your friend said you forgot this."

Bewildered, Faith opened the case. There, nestled in one of the little cups, was a small, fuzzy photo, the size of a pencil eraser.

"I found him!" Leslie yelled from the other side of the security check. "He was in the marching band. He played the tuba."

"He looks like a girl!" Faith yelled back, confused.

"He's standing behind her. You can see his ear!" Leslie answered.

The airline attendant spoke up impatiently. "We're ready when you are, ladies."

Faith and Kate moved down the jetway, their heads close together.

"Can you see anything else?"

"Only his ear. But it's a *nice* ear."

"How can you tell?"

"I just can."

"I think we need a magnifying glass."

"God no, then he'll look like Dumbo!"

The 747 sailed smoothly across the night sky. Inside the cabin, many of the passengers were sprawled asleep amid pillows and blankets. Others were reading or talking. At the rear of the plane the rest room door was slightly ajar. . . .

"I didn't have any time to get to the bank," Kate said, crammed with Faith and her wedding dress into the small rest room. The dress had spread to fill all the space around them.

Faith was kneeling on the closed toilet seat, her back to Kate, who was working to get the dress unbuttoned. "How much money do you have on you."

"About twenty-three dollars and sixty-seven cents."

They both exploded into laughter.

"Why do we think that's so funny?"

Faith grinned. "It could have something to do with the fact that what we're doing makes no sense at all."

"Oh, yeah, good point."

They both laughed again.

"We'll probably be horrified when we land and realize we're not in Pittsburgh."

"I doubt it."

"Yeah, I doubt it too." Kate giggled, then her eyes narrowed on the back of the wedding gown. "I want you to know that I'm trying my very best to get you out of this dress, but every time I get one button undone, ten more appear."

"Yeah, I know," she said, resi̶͟ keep at it. It's us against the dress̶

"Don't worry. No dress has ever gotten the better of me yet."

"Uh-huh . . . well . . ." Faith put her hand against the wall to steady herself. "I don't want to alarm you, but you should know that this dress may very well have come straight out of a Stephen King novel."

"What?"

"You know, like Christine, the car that wouldn't die?"

"What?"

"Never mind."

"What'd you tell Dwayne?"

"I left a message on his machine saying that I was going to a teacher's conference in New York City. I said it would calm my nerves before the wedding." She laughed, but this time there was a touch of seriousness in her laugh. "I promised I'd be back in time. How about you?"

"I left a note saying I would be up at the lake with my folks. Larry never calls me there."

There was a loud knock at the rest room door. "How long you going to be in there?" a masculine voice asked.

"We'll be out in a minute," Kate called. "There! It's unbuttoned."

"Thank goodness." She gathered up as much of the bulky skirt and petticoats as she could manage, then executed a series of careful, awkward maneuvers, once inexplicably hitting the flush button with her heel, sending her into a fit of giggles. Finally she managed to stand on the toilet seat, facing Kate. "We've got to be careful. This bathroom doesn't have much more room than a phone booth, and we could still drown."

"Drown? What are you talking about?"

"A phone booth. I'm talking about a phone booth."

"Oh—a phone booth." Kate looked at her worriedly.

She shrugged her shoulders out of the gown, wiggled, and pushed it down until it was billowing around her legs, then bent and lifted her feet one at a time while Kate pulled the wedding dress from under her.

A lace sleeve flew up and smacked Kate in the face and a poof of net threatened to smother her. She fought, but the sheer volume and weight of the dress pushed her back against the sink. She threw a bewildered look at Faith, who was standing on the toilet clad only in her underwear. "You know what? You may be right about this dress."

"I'm telling ya."

Kate shifted and maneuvered until, with great effort, she finally managed to wedge open the door and ease into the aisle of the plane, pulling the dress out behind her. Freed at last, the dress exploded in a tidal wave of lace, net, and buttons.

The man who had been waiting for them to emerge switched the baby he was carrying from one arm to the other and reached for the rest room door. But Faith managed to grab it first and slam it shut from the inside. "I'll be just a minute!"

The man looked at Kate. "How many people are in there?"

Kate smiled sweetly. "Not that many. It's just a small, very select party, really—only our closest friends."

The man was still trying to find words when Kate moved off down the aisle with the dress, its skirt indiscriminately assaulting the passengers in the aisle seats. "Is there someplace I can hang this?" she asked a flight attendant.

The tired-looking woman gazed curiously at the garment. "A wedding dress?"

"It's a long story."

"It's a long flight."

"Not that long, trust me."

The occupants of the plane had quieted. Most of the passengers had fallen asleep. Only a few still read or talked in low tones.

In her seat at the back of the plane Kate gazed out the dark window beside her and saw the faint image of herself staring back. It was like looking at a stranger.

Her life was made up of car pools, meals, laundry, soccer games, and doctor visits. It was a life that didn't have anything to do with the woman in the window, the woman who was leaving her husband and two sons behind and flying across a dark sea to a faraway place. And a strange thing was happening. With each mile that passed, the worries of being a wife and mother were dropping away from her.

Kate lifted her can of soda in a toast. "To be brave enough to be crazy."

Faith clunked her can against Kate's. "When we get there, I'm going to take a *vaporetto* to the Danieli Hotel. And I'll go through the doors and he's just going to be there. He'll see me and I'll see him."

Kate nodded sagely. "And his wife will see you."

"He won't be married. No. No. No." Her expression turned dreamy. "I'll call him on the house phone when I arrive. It will be late afternoon and beautiful—"

"He'll be taking his kids for a walk."

She was feeling very warm and cozy and with enough energy to fly to Venice without the plane, but she managed a faint frown for Kate. "He's not married, so he doesn't have kids."

"What if he's a priest?"

"He'd go to Rome. We'll meet on a terrace overlooking the Piazza San Marco. There will be a light breeze and"—she reached out her arm and stopped one of the flight attendants—"could you please give us two more cans of soda, thanks. . . .

"Oh, Kate, all my life I've waited for men to make the first move. Well, no more of that." She brought the flat of her hand down on the seat tray, making the soda cans dance and the man across the aisle start awake. "For once in my life I am finally taking charge of my own destiny. For once I'm . . ." She broke into a song. "For once in my life . . ."

Kate joined in, her voice harmonizing with Faith's. The plane glided across an almost full moon, and inside the dimly lit cabin Faith and Kate continued to sing, their voices gradually growing louder until they were really belting it out.

Across the aisle the man scrunched down in his seat and pulled a pillow around his ears.

4

Faith emerged from the Marco Polo Airport terminal in Venice and squinted at the light. A tiny person with a tiny hammer was running rampant in her head and her mouth tasted as if an entire army had marched through in dusty boots. She had the mother of all headaches, but she didn't care. She was in Venice!

She carried her various bags and her purse, plus the new garment bag she had just purchased in the airport gift shop with the wedding dress stuffed into it, temporarily tamed. But she didn't feel the weight. She was in *Venice*.

Kate slowly followed her out of the terminal, carefully putting one foot in front of the other. "The ground doesn't feel real steady, did you notice? Is it moving or is it just uneven?"

Faith glanced at her. "Well, there is that Leaning Tower of Pisa thing."

Kate nodded. "I'm so tired and jet-lagged. I can't believe you didn't tell me we had to switch planes."

"Would it have made a difference?"

"Yeah, it would have. Maybe I would have skipped one or two choruses. She gave the matter some thought. "Well, maybe one . . ."

"Look, we lost only three hours. And we're in *Europe*. Isn't it exciting?"

"Yeah, and insane." She took a closer look at the navy blue dress Faith had changed into on the plane. "Your dress is buttoned wrong."

She didn't even bother to glance down at the long line of buttons that ran down the front of her dress. "Tell me something. When exactly was it that buttons took over the world?"

"I haven't got a clue." Kate glanced vaguely around her. "Where are my sunglasses?"

Kate and Faith stood at the railing of the *vaporetto* as it glided over the wine-dark Adriatic toward Venice.

"My God, what is it?" Kate said softly, gazing in awe at the ancient and mystical city hovering in the distance.

"Venice," Faith said dreamily, leaning on the railing, staring at the same almost otherworldly scene looming before them. It was twilight, that magical time when day had not fully ended nor night yet begun. Golden light bathed everything and the city was painted in a wash of enchantment and romance. "La Serenissima, the Most Serene. Where people come looking for something they can't find anyplace else."

The pale pink-gold light shimmered on the buildings which were mirrored in the water. It was a fantasy from another time and Faith couldn't believe she was actually there.

"Just think about it, Kate. We're gliding across the Adriatic Sea to the labyrinths and gargoyles and crumbling palaces of Venice, *Italy*."

"It's nothing like Pittsburgh," Kate murmured apprehensively. A gondola passed, the couple on board locked in an embrace. She and Larry had once felt that kind of love, she remembered, the kind where they were the only two people on earth who mattered. Feeling a wistful tug of longing, her gaze followed the craft. "*Ow*! I was . . ." She caught Faith's eye and made a pinching motion with her fingers. Glancing around, she saw that the only person in the immediate vicinity was a young boy, the picture of innocence.

"Did you pinch me?"

"Non parlo inglese, Signorina."

Kate glared at him suspiciously. "You pinched me." She pulled the bill of his hat down over his eyes and gave a small, secret smile.

The *vaporetto* entered the Grand Canal, and suddenly they were in Venice. Faith drank in the sights as they floated past centuries-old palazzi, their crumbling façades rejuvenated in the gentle evening light. Candlelit windows cast shimmering patches of gold down onto the water and her imagination came alive. Inside those windows women in long gowns and men in flowing robes had once lived. There had been intrigues and secrets, passion and grand affairs.

"The home of Bernini, Casanova, Marco Polo," she murmured. "Inspiration of Wordsworth, Byron, Longfellow . . ."

"The Danieli," the driver called out as he steered the *vaporetto* up to the dock.

Faith stood motionless, gazing in wonder at the gracious and opulent façade of the Danieli, a fifteenth-century palazzo that was now a famous Venetian hotel. Its many balconies provided an atmosphere of another time, when Italian princesses and princes, along with noblemen and noblewomen, stood exactly where she was standing. Dock lanterns glowed, beckoning her into the sumptuous surroundings.

After all the frantic rushing and then the long trip to get there she was suddenly feeling weak at the knees. She had dreamed of coming to Venice. She had dreamed of meeting Damon Bradley. Half her dream had been fulfilled. And now she had only to step over the threshold of the hotel for the other half to come true.

"Wait a minute," Kate said, grabbing her arm as she started to the entrance. "This is a *Lifestyles* hotel."

"Really?"

She could tell by the dreamy look on Faith's face that she wasn't getting it. "As in

Lifestyles of the Rich and Famous? Of which we are neither. We can't afford this."

"Are you sure?"

"*Yes*. Cathy Lee Crosby stayed here."

Faith started off again but quickly stopped when she realized Kate wasn't moving. "It's going to be for only one night." Kate still didn't move. "They take credit cards." Kate was so still she looked like a statue. "We get frequent flyer miles."

Kate drew in a deep breath. "Okay."

A distinguished older man held the door for them. Faith eyed him intently as she passed him, then, as she moved forward, she gazed back over her shoulder at him.

"What?" Kate asked, watching her. "You think maybe that was him?"

Faith shook her head. "Certainly not." She'd know him when she saw him. How could she not? It was predestined.

Kate grabbed her arm. "My God, would you look at this *lobby*."

The old-world elegance of the lobby stunned and captivated her. The sight of vaulted ceilings, marble floors, and beautiful old rugs was everything she could have wished. A huge fireplace loomed on a far wall and everywhere there were exquisite vases

filled with towering fresh flower arrange-
ments. The scene was so romantic, so ripe
with possibilities. . . .

And the lobby bubbled with life. Sophisti-
cated-looking, elegant men sat, reading the
paper, lounging, smoking. There were women
too, but she barely noticed them. Damon
Bradley was there, somewhere. She only had
to find him.

Her eyes glistened with expectation. "Isn't
this wonderful?" she whispered.

"I've got to admit it's incredible."

"It's more than incredible. He could be
anywhere."

Kate nodded toward the front desk. "Let's
go see."

"*Buon giorno,*" the clerk said, greeting
them. He was a solidly built man in his late
fifties with a well-trimmed beard and an
aloof, slightly superior expression.

"Hello," Kate said. "Reservations for Faith
Corbett, please."

With a nod the clerk started punching the
keys of his computer. Kate pulled her credit
card out while Faith nervously scanned the
lobby.

"You will tell me if you see him, won't
you?"

Faith nodded absently. There were so many men in the lobby. Maybe she wouldn't know him. So, okay. Even if she didn't immediately recognize him, it didn't matter. He was here and at last she was going to meet him.

Kate turned back to the clerk with the credit card. "And put the room on this, please."

Faith heard the request and glanced at the card Kate was extending. It was an American Express card in the name of Lawrence Corbett. She looked at Kate, who gave a why-not? shrug.

Right, she thought. Why not, indeed? Why not hop on a plane and cross the ocean to find her destiny. Why not? And why not indulge herself in one more why-not? Mustering her courage, she said casually, "And could you please tell us what room Mr. Bradley is in?"

The clerk typed the name into his computer.

Faith watched, tense and excited. "God, I can't stand it, Kate. I'm just going to go right up to his room and explain it all."

"How? What are you going to say? Are you going to start with the Ouija board?"

"Probably. I don't know. Sure, why not? I'll just say—"

"I'm sorry," the clerk said. "Mr. Bradley has already checked out."

"Excuse me?" Faith said, turning back to him. "He can't have checked out. He just arrived today."

"Mr. Bradley left about a half hour ago. Would you prefer an interior or—"

"No, no, you don't understand. He couldn't have checked out—I was supposed to meet him here." It couldn't have been all for nothing. The Ouija board. Madame Divina. The telephone call. The trip. Her dreams . . .

"I'm very sorry. Perhaps you misunderstood?"

"Are you absolutely sure he's gone?" She was trying very hard not to panic. "Maybe you made a mistake. You must've made a mistake. Could you check again? Please? Sir?"

Americans. He barely refrained from rolling his eyes. Americans were so used to having things their way, they saw no reason why the world shouldn't fall in line with their wishes. But he knew his job. He was nothing if not professional. Politely he went through the pretense of checking the computer. "Sorry. Mr. Bradley is gone."

Faith stared at him, unable to accept what she was hearing.

Stubborn Americans. With a sigh he tried another approach. "Room 217," he said, reading off the screen, then turned to check the key box on the wall behind him. "His key has been returned. I'm afraid your friend has departed."

Stunned, Faith slowly moved away from the desk and started toward the front entrance.

"Which way did he go?" Kate asked the clerk.

"I don't know," he said politely but firmly. "We don't usually follow our guests."

Outside the Danieli, Faith approached the doorman. She'd come too far to give up, and this was her last chance. Pulling the yearbook photo from her wallet, she held the fuzzy little image out in front of him. "Have you seen this man? Which way did he go?"

"That's a girl."

"No, no, the ear *behind* the girl."

The doorman took another look at the photograph and burst out laughing. *Americans.* God, they were so funny.

Faith's expression darkened. "I'm *serious!*"

He immediately stopped laughing. Americans might make him laugh, but they gave really nice tips.

Pointing in the distance, he rattled something off in Italian.

Faith took off running in the direction he pointed—along the street, across a bridge, toward the canal. She had to find him!

She arrived at the dock out of breath and frantically scanned the people boarding a *vaporetto*. A woman brushed past her, then a man. Someone else jostled against her, knocking her hand. The little photograph fluttered to the ground. She reached down for it just as a man wearing a pair of shiny brown loafers stepped down on it. She grabbed at the man's leg and missed. She grabbed again, and this time she got it, much to the surprise of the man wearing the loafers.

"Excuse me, sir. I'm sorry, but I think there's something that belongs to me stuck the bottom of your shoe."

Confused, the man looked down at her.

"Do you mind if I just—"

She took the shoe and gently lifted it, turning it inward. Sure enough, the tiny image was still miraculously perched there. With a small triumphant sound she licked a finger and picked it off the shoe like a crumb. "Thank you—"

Suddenly a big gust of wind came up,

whisking the little likeness off her finger and into the Grand Canal. She stood and watched helplessly as the tiny photo washed away in the swirl of dark water.

"What was it?" the man asked curiously.

"My destiny."

"Two eleven," Faith said, walking slowly down the second floor corridor, counting the room numbers on the doors. "Two thirteen . . ."

"I don't think we should be wandering around up here," Kate said in a whisper.

"We're guests. We're entitled to be here."

"Not on this floor."

"What difference does it make?"

"Our room is not on this floor. It makes sense to me. Why doesn't it make sense to you?" Kate jumped as a maid passed by, wheeling a squeaky cart.

"Here it is," Faith said happily, stopping in front of a door. "Room 217."

"What if somebody's in there?"

"There's nobody in there. He just checked out an hour ago. C'mon, Kate," Faith said beseechingly. "Maybe his room hasn't been cleaned yet. Maybe there's something in there that might help us."

"I'm not breaking into anybody's room."

"Yesterday you didn't plan to fly to Venice either."

"Yesterday I was sane."

"Yeah, me too. *Excuse me,*" she called to the maid who had stopped her cart three doors down.

A minute later, having accepted a wad of dollar bills, the maid was opening the door to Room 217.

Faith walked in, almost breathless with excitement. "Just think, he was *here.* He breathed this air, he touched this—" She broke off as the condition of the room sank in.

Placing her hands on her hips, Kate surveyed the scene. "It looks like a cyclone hit in here. So far I'd say we're looking for a rich slob."

Faith spotted a wastebasket in the corner and hurried over to it. She picked it up and peered in. "A Butterfinger wrapper!" She pulled the wrapper out, as thrilled as if she'd found a handful of diamonds.

Kate wasn't as easily charmed. "Okay, so he's a rich, possibly fat slob."

"But don't you see? He has a sweet tooth. So do I. It's something we have in common."

Kate shook her head. "And you wonder why I worry about you."

Hopefully she studied the wrapper. "Maybe there are fingerprints on it."

"We're not looking to arrest the man, Faith, we're trying to locate him."

She dropped the wrapper and dug through the wastebasket again. She found more Butterfinger wrappers and one other piece of paper. Saying a silent prayer, she unfolded it. "Saints be praised, it's a telephone message!" She paused, staring hard at it. "Only . . . only . . . it's in Italian."

"Well, then, offhand, I'd say we lucked out."

"How?"

"This city just happens to be full of people who speak the language."

Faith looked at Kate. "Why didn't I think of that?"

"Honey, you haven't been thinking right since—"

"Never mind. Come on, we're getting close."

"Uh-huh."

Faith handed the precious piece of paper to the same clerk they had spoken with earlier.

He examined the message critically, then looked at the two women with a raised brow. "This is a phone number in Rome. You would like me to call this number and what . . . . ?"

Faith glanced at Kate, momentarily bereft of even a clue as to what to do.

Kate shrugged. "Just ask for Damon Bradley."

Faith's brain slowly began to work again. "Right. And ask whoever answers the phone if they know Mr. Bradley or where we might find him. *Please*."

With a sigh the clerk began to dial. *"Un momento."* After a moment he spoke into the phone. "Ai Monastèro?" He paused, listening. *"Va bène."*

Faith's hand flew to her heart. "A monastery?"

"My God," Kate said. "He *is* a priest."

The clerk put his hand over the mouthpiece. "Shhh, it's a store. In Rome." He spoke into the phone. *"Sì. Sto cercando Damon Bradley?"* He paused, listening. *"Sì. Sì. Grazie. Ciao."* He hung up and returned the piece of paper to Faith. "He said he thinks some woman he works with knows him. Her name's Anna. But she won't be in till tomorrow."

Faith turned to Kate. "We gotta get to Rome."

"Rome?" Kate's eyes widened in disbelief. "My God, Faith, I am so tired. This is like one of those sleep-deprivation experiments I read about in psych class."

"Sleep is highly overrated."

"Not to a woman with two boys."

5

Tuscany at dawn resembled an old Renaissance painting, Faith reflected as she drove the rented red Fiat along a small road. The morning was idyllic, opening up before her and allowing her glimpses of vast vineyards and occasional olive groves. Here and there she could also see a crumbling farmhouse dotting the gently undulating hills.

Any other time she would have been enchanted at the wonder of it, but she was tired and she and Kate, stuffed with their suitcases into the tiny car, were getting on each other's nerves.

"How would anyone ever know?" Kate asked, bemused, studying the enormous map hat spread over her lap and nearly blocked the windshield. "We arrive in Italy and all of a sudden it's showboat general."

"It's called *sciopero generale*," Faith corrected. "It's a national strike day. All workers get out their grievances in one day. And it's not such a bad idea." She glanced into the rearview mirror and saw the garment bag that held the wedding dress blocking the mirror. "Will you please try to beat down that wedding dress so I can see?"

Kate twisted around and gave the bag a couple of vicious swats, but the bag remained as voluminous as ever. She straightened back around. "Everybody on strike? The whole country just shuts down for twenty-four hours? And you think that's a good idea? What kind of country is it? Buses, trains, planes, boats—nobody shows up for work."

Faith slowed the car and turned onto an even smaller road. "The point is"—she hit the steering wheel in frustration—"we're on the *wrong* road. We've been on the wrong road for an hour."

Kate scanned the map. "No, the point is, it's looping. It's looping right around here and it's going to loop us right back to this freeway or turnpike or whatever the hell they call it."

They crested a hill and the pavement of the road turned into dirt. "Uh-oh." Faith slowed the car and squinted at the signs ahead. There were eight different signs with eight alternative routes, including Roma, which pointed in two different directions.

"So which way do we loop, Kate? Right or left?"

"Right," she said, concentrating hard on the map. "Left. Right."

"Okay." Faith stepped on the accelerator, guiding the Fiat right, then left, then right.

"I told you a liter was less than a gallon," Kate said, slamming the door of the Fiat so hard, the little car rocked.

Faith sat fuming in the car as she watched Kate walk away. "We would've had enough gas to get us there if you hadn't gotten us lost. Besides, a kilometer is less than a mile."

"Right. Less than a mile. So we should've been able to cover more of them."

"Are you such a know-it-all at home too?" she called out the window. "Is that you problem?"

Too tired and upset to answer, Kate dropped down on the ground, leaned back against a low stone wall, and gazed at the lovely rolling hills before her. Overhead a bird cawed. In the distance was the Tuscan town of San Gimignano with its high walls and medieval towers. The view looked like a picture postcard, she thought, taking a swig from the bottle of wine she had brought from the car.

Behind her she heard the car door slam. "Ancient Italy," she murmured, and gave a little wave of her hand toward the medieval towers when Faith walked up beside her. "God, what time is it in Pittsburgh?" She rubbed her forehead. "Faith, I'm sorry I got us lost."

"No, I'm sorry I'm so edgy." She dropped down beside her. "I'm afraid I'm losing him."

Kate nodded understandingly. "I didn't tell Larry I was going to the lake with the kids. I told him I was leaving him."

Faith's head whipped around. "Leaving him? Why?"

"I think he's having an affair."

"*Larry?*" she asked, shocked. "How do you know? Did he tell you?"

"No."

"Did you see him with her?"

"No."

"Then how do you know?"

"I just know." Tears flooded Kate's eyes. She tried to hold them back, but she had been trying to hold them back for too long. Breaking down, she began to cry.

Faith put her arm around her. "Oh honey, don't cry. I'm sure it's not true."

After a few minutes Kate wiped the tears from her cheeks and sniffed. "It's true."

"Listen, do you remember in junior high when I had that Halloween party? We were playing Twister. And it landed on the right hand red, and there was only one red spot left. You reached for it, but you started to fall. And instead of taking it, Larry reached out to catch you. He let you win. Larry never let anybody win. That's when I knew he was a goner."

Still sniffing, Kate reached for a twig and began to idly doodle in the dirt. "That was a long time ago."

"And you know what I thought then, Kate? I thought, I hope someday I'll have somebody who loves me that much." She paused, then confessed, "I still hope that."

Kate smiled ruefully. "That you'll find someone who'll let you win at Twister?"

"I *know* he loves you. I know he would kill tigers for you."

Tossing the stick away, Kate looked at her, her eyes full of doubt.

Faith nodded solemnly. "He would."

The sun was warm and a gentle wind stirred through the grass and trees of the Italian countryside. Kate dropped her head onto Faith's lap and closed her eyes. As Faith began to gently stroke her head, a tear slipped from beneath Kate's lashes and streamed down her cheek.

A patient lay in a reclining chair with his feet in the air. Wearing rubber gloves, Dwayne carefully prepared a plaster mold of one foot. Hearing a tapping on his office window, he looked up and saw Larry waving for him to come out into the corridor. He held up a plaster-covered finger. "Just a minute." He turned his best professional smile on his patient, a worried-looking middle-aged man. "Excuse me for a moment, Mr. Randolph. I'll be right back." He walked out into the hall. "What?"

"Something's up with Faith and Kate."

"I know. I've had that feeling too, but wha do you think it is? I've been worried. I jus haven't been sure what I should be worried about."

Larry shook his head. "Something's no right. I'm telling you I'm very suspicious. The two of them, both gone, a week before the wedding. I know those two. Something's up."

"I called the principal's office. There's no conference."

"Ha! They're together. I *knew* it. Bu where?"

"Good question. And why?" He glanced through the window at his patient. Mr. Ran dolph was looking even more worried. He gave him a reassuring smile.

"Kate left me a note that she's leaving me Of course, I didn't believe it. You don't run away from your husband with his sister, you know? I mean, how stupid is that?"

"Yeah, I guess, but I don't get it. Why would your wife just up and leave suddenly Hey, are you . . . I mean . . . you haven't been fooling around, have you?"

"No, no, no." Larry glanced away. "Kate hardly leaves our block. Where would she go?"

The sun beat down on the countryside, shimmering over the land, making heat waves dance on the road. Faith slowly came awake. She'd been dreaming of Damon Bradley. In her dream he had been everything she had ever expected he would be—charming, funny, gallant, strong, sexy. Unfortunately he had had no face.

She peered through her lashes to see a nun shaking the last drops of gasoline from a gas can into the Fiat's tank. She closed her eyes, then opened them again. The nun was still there. Where was Kate?

Disoriented, she sat up just in time to see the nun climbing into a convertible with two other nuns and an elegantly dressed woman driver. Maybe she was still dreaming.

Suddenly Kate appeared from the other side of the road. "Thank you, Sisters!"

With a cheery wave they roared away.

"God," Faith said, "the Catholic Church is even richer than I thought."

Kate turned and gave her the thumbs-up sign. "We're saved."

Faith maneuvered the Fiat around the Colosseum and through a tough left turn, then cut over four lanes of traffic. A cacophony of beeping horns awarded her efforts.

"Rome is like the Daytona 500 without the rules," she muttered.

Kate was studying the map in her lap. "There are rules, but I think you have to be Italian to know them."

Faith braked, narrowly managing to avoid a collision. "Have you noticed? Italians have no nerves when it comes to driving."

"It's all that wine they drink."

"Well, it's been hours since we've had any, so let's park this sucker and take local transportation."

"No, no, let's just keep going. We'll find *Ai Monastèro* eventually."

"Kate, all my life I've believed in destiny. I still do, but now I'm beginning to understand that destiny might have a time limit. Like for instance the day of my wedding, ya know? I don't have time for *eventually*."

"I see your point," Kate said. "Take a right. The Euro Rent-A-Car should be just around the corner. We'll get a taxi from there."

Minutes later Faith was instructing a taxi driver. *"Ai Monastèro, per favore."*

The cab made a quick U-turn and came to

halt on the opposite side of the street. There, a sign read AI MONASTÈRO.

"See?" Kate said. "We were really close."

The driver smiled and held out his hand.

A hushed environment reminiscent of a monastery reigned inside the store. Leather sandals, bags, and gloves made by monks were prominently displayed. Adorning one of the counters was a soignee Italian woman with long, lustrous hair, thick lashes, and great dark eyes.

"Hello?" Faith said, almost whispering. "Uh, *parla inglese?*"

The woman gave her a demure smile. *"Un poco."*

"Thank God. I'm looking for Anna?"

"I am Anna."

She broke into a huge smile of joy and extended her hand. "Anna, I'm Faith," she said, speaking louder now. "You don't know how happy I am to meet you." The woman took her hand tentatively, then released it. "You see, I'm trying to find someone, and I was thinking that maybe somebody here—well, you—might know him. His name is Damon Bradley?"

Anna's eyes narrowed. "Damon Bradley."

"Yes!" she said, thrilled. "You *do* know him?"

Anna slammed her expresso down on the counter. *"È un porco!"*

"Excuse me."

Anna started ranting in Italian and making wild gestures with her hands. Faith grabbed her Italian dictionary and began to frantically flip through it.

Kate walked up behind her. "What's she saying?"

"I don't know. It's something about a pig." She looked at Anna.

Hearing the commotion, the proprietor came rushing out from the recesses of the store. He was tall, handsome, impeccably dressed with an interesting touch of gray at his temples. And instead of looking at Faith he looked at Kate. "May I be of assistance?"

"My friend is looking for someone, and she thinks this woman knows him. His name is Damon Bradley."

Faith gave up on the dictionary. "Could you ask her if she knows how I might reach him? If she has a telephone number for him? An address?"

He turned to Anna and listened as she

continued to rant and rave. Occasionally he would nod. Finally he turned back. "He called her from Venice, and he thinks she's going to meet him at the Sabatini's Restaurant tonight in the Piazza di Santa Maria in Trastevere, but she—"

"Hah!" Anna hit her inner elbow with the edge of her other hand.

The proprietor eyed the obscene gesture and discreetly cleared his throat. "—has a prior commitment."

Faith was ecstatic. "That's it. That's it! That's all I need to know." She grabbed the hands of Anna and the proprietor in turn. "Bless you, thank you, thank you." In celebration, she threw her arms around Kate and practically did a soft-shoe toward the door.

The proprietor watched them for a moment, taking in their suitcases. Then he spoke, again to Kate. "You are looking for a place to stay, no?"

"As a matter of fact—"

"Perhaps I can help." He crossed to her and with a great flourish took her hand and kissed it. "I am Giovanni. And you are?"

"Kate." Amused, she retrieved her hand and looked down at it. A handsome, suave Italian man had just kissed her hand. . . .

"Kate." He beamed at her as he said her name and something inside her melted a little. "I know a *pensione bellissimo*—is very close."

"C'mon, Kate," Faith said impatiently, standing at the door. "Let's go."

Kate turned on her. *"Faith!"*

"What?"

"I am jet-lagged. Hung over. I haven't eaten enough food or slept for two days. *I want a room!*"

"Oh. Okay. Why didn't you say so?"

Kate gave Giovanni a smile. "You were saying . . ."

He took her arm. "Allow me . . ."

Giovanni guided them to the *Pensione Divino Amore*. It was a charming little inn with a tiled fountain tinkling in its terra-cotta courtyard. After carrying their things into the hotel, he pulled Kate aside.

"I must leave town for two days," he said apologetically. "I must go to my other shop in Milano. Was unavoidable. But, day after tomorrow"—he paused to give what he was about to say greater importance—"I return. It is my hope that you will be here."

With great tenderness he placed the room key in her hand, then held his own there slightly longer than necessary.

Kate gazed up into his dark eyes, eyes that plainly said he saw her as a woman, not as a mother or the woman who washed his clothes or cooked his meals. A woman. A *desirable* woman. And right then and there she decided that she was either very hungry, more sleep deprived than she had originally thought, or she was falling in love.

Or maybe it was a little of all three.

"I told you that you were going to need an adapter for your hair dryer," Kate said as she and Faith emerged from the taxi in the Piazza di Santa Maria in Trastevere. "That's why it sparked and ran at double speed."

Faith gazed at the front of the Sabatini. "I'm nervous."

"No kidding?" Kate grinned. "Is that why you're not listening to me?"

Faith smoothed a sweaty palm down the long, slim red velvet dress she was wearing. "Do I look okay?"

"You look gorgeous. I'm glad I packed it."

"Are you sure it's okay?" she asked, still

uncertain. "I always thought it was too tight. Or bare. Or something."

"It's perfect. And you look perfect too."

She groaned and adjusted the red velvet stole around her shoulders. "Why couldn't we just have arranged marriages in America? Everything would be so much simpler."

"You're right. At least that way you could spend the rest of your life blaming your parents instead of yourself."

"Sounds good to me."

"No, it doesn't."

"No, it doesn't," she agreed with a rueful smile.

Kate touched her arm. "Hey, listen, just remember, whatever happens tonight, you're going to be okay."

"You're right. Nothing terrible is going to happen. I'm not going to make a fool of myself. Damon Bradley is not going to look at me like I'm crazy. I hope. Let's go."

The restaurant was everything Faith could have wanted for the momentous occasion. Candlelight glowed, softening angles and lines, and laughter and conversation filtered out until there was nothing left but romance and a sea of frescoes, flowers, crystal, and silver.

She gazed expectantly at the scene. A whole lifetime of waiting, searching, hoping, and it had all come down to this one moment. Now she only had to find him.

A variety of men acknowledged her presence with typical Italian admiration. They smiled at her, they glanced, one even winked. But others appeared oblivious of her. And Damon Bradley could be any of them. Or none of them.

"Let's get a drink," she said through her frozen smile. "We're on vacation."

Kate followed her to the bar. "Aren't you going to ask the maître d' if he's here?"

"White wine, please," she said to the man behind the bar. It felt as if steel bands had clamped around her chest. It was taking a great deal of her energy and concentration just to breathe. "I, uh, sort of wanted to wait to see if maybe he'd notice me first."

There were so many men in the restaurant, but they were all acting more or less normal. None of them was staring at her as if he was trying to place her, as though he might have known her in another life or recognized her on some kind of subconscious level.

As soon as the bartender placed the wine

in front of her, she reached for it and took a sip.

Kate was staring at her with disbelief. "You've trailed the man halfway around the world and now you're gonna play *hard to get*?"

"Yeah, well . . ." She couldn't defend or justify her actions, because even to her they were beginning not to make sense. She was going on gut instinct now, and it was beyond her to explain. Taking another sip of the wine, she glanced around the room one final time, then sighed. "Okay, okay. I guess we've waited long enough. I think you better ask the maître d' if he's here."

"Now you're talking."

With her heart in her throat she watched as Kate slipped off the stool and approached the maître d'. Then she deliberately turned her back. If Damon Bradley really was here, she needed to compose herself. She couldn't be an emotional wreck when she presented herself to him. She needed to be calm. She needed to impress him with her logic and reason regarding their joint destiny. Yes, that's what she needed to do.

And if he wasn't here, she still needed to compose herself. She needed to remind herself that this trip, this quest, was after all nothing more than a lark. Her original intention when she had raced out to the airport had been only to get a look at him. In a matter of days she would be marrying Dwayne. Good-as-gold Dwayne. Doctor Dwayne. She downed a large gulp of the wine.

Kate rushed back to her side. "He's heeeeeeerrrre. . . ."

Faith's composure disappeared. "Oh, my God." She glanced nervously around. "Where?"

"He's sitting inside right by the door. He's on the right-hand side with his back to us. He's wearing a navy jacket. If you turn around, you can see part of his right elbow."

Faith didn't move. "Is he looking at us?"

Kate glanced over her shoulder. "Nope."

As casually as she could manage, she took a peek, then her hand flew to her heart. "Oooooo, I can see his sleeve!" She tried to breathe but couldn't. She tried again and finally managed to get a small but reassuring amount of air into her lungs. Suddenly she felt as awkward and unpolished as a twelve-year-old. "I guess I should just go over and introduce myself, huh?"

Kate nodded. "That's definitely what you should do."

She started to get up, but then quickly sat back down.

"What is it now?"

She looked at Kate uncertainly. "Who do I say I am?"

"Faith Corbett. It's a good name. Stick with it. If you want me to, I'll write it on your hand so that you don't forget it."

"Faith Corbett. Right." She finished her glass of wine.

Across the restaurant a waiter placed a check on the table of a booth. A masculine hand reached out and picked up the check and after a moment returned it with the money on top.

"Okay," Faith said. "I know what I'm going to say."

"Good."

"Yeah, good . . . okay . . ." A gigantic portion of self-doubt seized her. "You don't think he's gonna think I'm too aggressive?"

"Faith honey, so far you've traveled four thousand miles. What's fifteen more feet?"

"Right. Okay. It's meant to be, right?" At Kate's reassuring smile, Faith drew in a deep breath. "This is it."

She slipped off the barstool and strode purposefully toward him, focused only on that special arm. And with each step a little more of his arm came into view until she could see that he was wearing a navy blazer.

Only a few more yards . . .

Two waiters arrived at a table between her and the booth, brandishing huge, flaming plates. With great flourish and fanfare they set about to serve the table.

Trying to keep the booth in sight, she leaned left, then right, but the waiters continued to block her view.

A man in a blue blazer moved toward the exit.

Still determined, she reversed course and hustled around the bar, taking the long way around to Damon's booth.

The man in the blue blazer walked out of the restaurant.

With a mumbled apology Faith squeezed past a cart and ducked under the cane of an elderly gentleman climbing to his feet.

Finally she reached Damon's booth.

Empty.

She whirled. *"Kaaaaaate!"*

The whole restaurant turned to look at the shrieking woman.

Kate jumped to her feet and raced after Faith.

6

Faith bolted out the door just in time to catch a glimpse of a man in a navy jacket disappearing across the street into the twilight.

She tore across the street after him. A car swerved to avoid hitting her. Another driver laid on his horn and made an obscene gesture out the window. But Faith didn't even bother to say excuse me. Her gaze was fixed on the man's arm as he turned the corner.

She raced around the same corner and found herself in a bustling plaza.

Where was he?

She looked right and left.

There were so many people.

Trying not to panic, she stared hard at the

crowd. Colors blurred. The people began to all look alike.

Focus.

At last she saw a man wearing a blue blazer in the distance, heading up a set of stone stairs to another level of the square.

She set out after him, up the stairs and into an alley, past old shops and artists' warrens, beneath garlands of laundry strung from building to building, dodging around an amorous couple.

She was gaining on him. She was—

She was jerked to a standstill.

"Wha—?" Her high heel was caught in a subway grate. She tugged at it, but it refused to give.

Oh, God, he was going to get away.

She stepped out of the shoe, stripped off her other one, and darted off again, the ends of the red velvet stole dancing against her legs.

She was concentrating so hard on the man in the navy blazer directly ahead of her that she didn't even notice when she bumped into another man who was wearing a white shirt and carrying a navy blazer.

But he noticed her.

And he stopped to watch as she cut

through the crowds. Then, glancing back where she'd come from, he saw her shoe, still caught in the grate.

$\mathbb{K}$ate paced back and forth in front of the fountain in the Piazza di Santa Maria in Trastevere. It was dark now and she was beginning to worry about Faith. Had she finally found Damon Bradley? She hoped so.

She sympathized and understood her friend's quest. Deep inside she supposed she also still believed in romantic dreams and love. She knew she certainly had at one time. But dealing with the everyday details of raising a family and the minutiae of just plain living took a great deal of effort. Larry worked hard at his roofing business and she had the house and the kids to deal with. In the past few years there had seemed to be less and less time for romantic dreams.

But she missed the romance in her life. She missed having Larry look at her in that special way, his eyes glowing with love and laughter. Faith had said Larry would kill tigers for her. She wasn't sure that was true anymore.

Just then she saw Faith entering the piazza.

"What happened?" Kate asked worriedly as Faith limped over to the fountain and collapsed on its edge. "Where's your other shoe?"

Faith waved her hand in a vague gesture. "In a subway grate somewhere back there. I had the other one off for a while, but then my feet started to hurt so I decided to put it back on because I thought I should at least protect one foot, ya know?"

"I gather you lost Damon Bradley?"

"I had him in my sights all the way. Then I darted around a corner just as an outdoor ballet of *Petruschka* was letting out and suddenly there I was, caught in the middle of all these people. A great throng of them . . ."

Kate sat down beside her. "So you lost him."

She nodded glumly. "Lost him."

"Well, look, honey, don't let yourself get too down. Nobody can say we didn't try." Faith looked as if she had gone into a trance, Kate noted with concern. "Don't be upset, okay? You tried. You tried your best. I mean, when you think about it, there's gotta be a better way than destiny. You shouldn't have to literally chase someone halfway around the world and then chase them some more through alleys and piazzas and what-not. You know? I mean, if destiny has someone in mind for you, destiny should at least help out a little. Maybe put the person in your path once or twice, don't you think? *Faith?*"

"What? Okay, here's what I think. We rent a truck, or a car, either one, and we set up a loudspeaker, and we drive through the surrounding areas, and we page him."

Kate's mouth fell open. "You're serious, aren't you?"

"Perfectly." For the first time she noticed Kate's dumbfounded expression. "What? Or, hey, how about skywriting."

"Excuse me, were you looking for this?"

Faith glanced up and saw a man standing there with her other shoe in his hand. "Oh, thank you," she said, and reached for it. "Now, Kate—"

"Allow me." Without giving a thought as to what he was doing, he knelt and placed the shoe on her foot. To a certain extent, kneeling in front of a woman was a small part of his business. But kneeling at this particular woman's feet had nothing to do with busi-

ness, nor had following her. He had been acting on a compulsion he couldn't explain.

He finished placing the shoe on her foot,
then gazed up at her. And he received a
shock. She had *amazing* eyes. They were
large and a beautiful liquid brown. But more
than that, they were deep, fathomless, as if
he could see all the way to her soul. And he
saw something in them, a light, a hope, a
yearning that matched something in him.
And to top it off, she had the face of an angel.

Faith barely looked at him. "Thanks very
much. So, Kate, what do you think?"

"That was really sweet," Kate said,
charmed by his actions.

Faith frowned, not understanding what
she was talking about. "I meant about my
idea."

"I think it's time we got some professional
help."

She nodded. "Like a detective."

"Like a psychiatrist."

"How's a psychiatrist gonna find him?"
She followed Kate's gaze and saw the man,
still kneeling in front of her. "Thank you." Her
tone was dismissive.

"Size eight B," he said.

"I beg your pardon?"

"Your shoe size. Eight B."

"Yes. Exactly. How'd you know?"

"In the shoe biz, the foot is our naked canvas. You're wearing American Eagles." Playfully he switched to his best sales-pitch tone. "They're impetuous, fun, elegant. And I hope they bring you to whatever it was you were running after just then."

"Her destiny," Kate said, mildly fascinated by him.

"Do you believe in destiny?" Faith asked him. "I can't convince her. I have come all the way from Pittsburgh to Venice, over the hills of Tuscany to Rome to—"

"Find your destiny. And have you found it?"

No, she thought with a sigh, she hadn't found it. But she couldn't give up now. "Excuse me, I have to go buy a book and look up every hotel in Rome." She jumped up and moved off.

He and Kate automatically followed.

"So, what's up with your friend?" he asked, keeping an eye on her red-velvet-clad body. He'd laugh at himself, trailing after a strange woman this way, if he didn't feel such a serious urgency to follow her. Ironically she wasn't even seeing him and all he could see was her.

Kate shrugged. "My friend has lost her mind."

"So why does she have to look up every hotel in Rome?"

"To find the man of her dreams. That's what she's doing. She thinks he's here. Even though she's never met him. Even though she's never laid *eyes* on him."

"No, seriously, what's she doing?"

Kate looked at him. "That's what she's doing."

"Oh." Well, he reflected wryly, what she was doing wasn't any crazier than what he was doing—chasing after a woman who was chasing after another man. It wasn't smart, but he couldn't seem to stop himself.

He had heard of love at first sight, of course. Who hadn't? Until now, though, he hadn't had firsthand experience with it. But he had looked into those gorgeous eyes of hers and his heart had scored a direct hit.

He had never felt like this before. Ever. It was how he imagined being struck by lightning would feel—electrifying and involving every one of his senses. The total, all-consuming need to include himself in her life was outside his experience, but he wasn't about to fight it. If she had her way, she would disappear out of his life. If he had his way, she would stay.

He caught up with the two women. "So what's wrong with her searching for the man of her dreams?"

Hearing the last part of his conversation, Faith slowed and smiled at him. At last, someone who thought like she did. "Really? You think it's—"

"Wonderful." Quite subtly, quite deliberately, he maneuvered himself between the two women. "Only, if you've never met this guy, how do you know he's perfect for you?"

Kate shook her head. "Don't ask. Really. You're better off not knowing."

"Were they pen pals?"

"No, they were not."

"Is he some kind of celebrity or something?"

"Of course not," Faith said, and darted over to a kiosk to buy the book.

He yelled after her. "Did he do some anonymous good deed?"

Kate let out an exasperated sigh directed at Faith. "She got his name from a Ouija board when she was a kid." She held her hands out, palms up. "What can I tell you?"

"What's his name?"

Faith came skipping back, excitedly waving her book. "I got one. Let's get to a phone."

Kate reluctantly fell into step beside her.

"Wait a minute." He flung his jacket over his shoulder and hurried after them. "Will you be staying in Rome long?"

With but a single thought in her mind she opened the book and began scanning it.

He looked at Kate. "Will you?"

"No. In fact, we're not even supposed to be here."

Faith glanced up, saw a taxi in the distance, and executed a piercing two-finger whistle, and at the exact same moment he did the same.

"Maybe I can help you track him down," he said anxiously. He was used to thinking fast on his feet, but with this woman he needed to think even faster. "I speak a little Italian. And I have a friend who works at the embassy. Maybe we could—"

She waved at the cab. "Thank you, but this is a personal matter."

He was well aware that there were always

consequences to everything a person said or did, but in this instance he was willing to take whatever risk necessary. Desperate situations called for desperate measures. "What's his name? I'll look into it for you. What's your number? I could give you a call. . . ."

The cab slowed to a stop in front of them and Kate went around to the other side to get in. Faith glanced at him.

"Look, it's very nice of you to offer, but—" She tried to reach for the door, but he was standing in the way.

He racked his brain. What could he do or say to keep her from walking out of his life? He needed a sign, *something.* "Just tell me his name."

Anything to get rid of him. "Damon Bradley."

He stared at her, stunned. "But, that's . . . *I'm* Damon Bradley."

For the first time he had her complete and undivided attention. Everything around her seemed to grow very quiet as the words he had spoken repeated in her head. He was carrying a jacket, she noticed. A *navy blue* jacket. She looked up into his eyes. They were velvet brown, soulful, sensitive. And they were the eyes of a man who dreamed.

Somewhere above her she heard the faint rustle of the wind through the trees. "You're . . ."

He nodded, as amazed as she was. And somewhat embarrassed.

And then she fainted, straight into his arms.

In answer to the persistent ringing of his doorbell, Dwayne opened his front door.

Larry strode in, his face unshaved, his eyes bloodshot. "Have you heard from them?"

"God, Larry, you look awful. When's the last time you had a good meal or a full night's sleep?"

"Never mind. Just tell me. Have you heard from them?"

"Not a goddamn word." He turned and retraced his steps into the den, where he had been watching a basketball game on television. "Come on. I've got some food in the other room."

In the den he gestured toward the Big Mac and fries he had neatly arranged on a dinner plate, along with a milk shake he had placed in a coffee-cup holder. "I'll share. Want some fries or something? Or I've got some stuff in the freezer you could nuke."

Larry shook his head. He was too upset about Kate's leaving him to think about food. His imagination had been running wild, and all kinds of scenarios had occurred to him, none of them good. "Jesus, it's been forty-eight hours."

"You're telling me. How could she do this to me?"

"How could she do this to *you*? I'm married. We're talking about my wife here. The mother of my children."

Dwayne dropped onto the couch in front of his food. "It's getting embarrassing. The caterer's been calling. The florist's been calling."

Larry gazed worriedly out the window at the Pittsburgh skyline. "How is she living? She never carries any cash."

"Aw, shit."

Alarmed Larry swung back to Dwayne. *"What?"*

Dwayne gestured to the television. "What the hell kind of call is that?"

Full and mysterious, the moon hung in the sky above Rome, bathing the Tiber and all its surroundings in its brilliant light.

She had never experienced a more enchanting night, Faith thought, walking beside Damon as they approached an ancient bridge that spanned the river. It was an utterly perfect night to be with the man whom she had dreamed of meeting practically her whole life. *Damon Bradley.* She could hardly believe that she had finally found him and that she was walking beside him under a spellbindingly radiant moon. But now, after all the time and all the effort, she felt awkward and unsure.

"I was—"

"I was—" he said, speaking at the same time.

"What?" Damon asked, deferring to her.

"Oh, nothing," she said, deferring to him. "What were you going to say?"

"Nothing. I was just—only . . ." He trailed off. God, she was adorable. Without knowing why, he laughed, but it was okay because she laughed with him. He had walked beneath a full Italian moon before. He had also known his share of women. But this night, this woman—*Faith*—was extraordinary. "Is it too cool for you?"

"Oh, no, no, not at all. It's perfect." She idly adjusted the stole around her shoulders. There could have been snow on the ground and she wouldn't notice, not tonight. "Are you? Too cool?"

"No . . . no."

On the bridge now, they stopped and looked down at the dark water of the Tiber.

"Isn't it amazing?"

"Isn't it amazing?"

Faith laughed and he laughed with her. "Our minds are working together."

"Yeah," he said softly, tenderly, happily.

"I was just thinking," Faith said as they continued across the bridge, their steps matching perfectly. "You're from Boston, I'm from Pittsburgh, we're here in Rome. Do you know how close we came to never, ever meeting?"

He nodded. "You know, there's this poem by Goethe, about two people who are in different places, but they hear the same bird singing . . . or something like that."

"I know that one," she said, excited that he would think of the poem. "Who knows? Perhaps the same bird echoed through both of us, yesterday, separate, in the evening. . . ."

"Yeah. Exactly."

"Except it was Rilke."

"Are you sure?"

"I'm an English teacher."

He smiled at her and in a haze of happiness she smiled back.

The sounds of a saxophone drifted across the night. She looked toward the other side of the bridge and saw a musician under a street-lamp. He was playing "Some Enchanted Evening."

By mutual, unspoken consent the two of them made their way over. Faith wasn't even sure her feet touched the ground. The song added magic to the already magical night. Days before she had heard the same song and wished for the romance it promised. And now, here she was, with the man she had been told was her soul mate. The enthrallingly beautiful notes wound through the air and wrapped around her. Slowly she lost her self-consciousness and began to sway and snap her fingers. The musician picked up the song's tempo. Damon tapped his foot and she clapped along.

Then, much to her delight, Damon did a few steps of an old dance.

"The Bus Stop," he said, and grinned when she joined him in the steps. After a minute he called out, "The Hustle." They danced in perfect sync, mimicking each other's movements. Periodically he called out another dance. The Bump. The Swim. The Hitchhiker.

"The Hokey-Pokey!" Faith said.

Damon cracked up laughing, and when

he put his right hand in, he dropped a coin into the musician's cup, then he slipped his arm around her and they danced away.

"'You put your right foot in,'" she sang. "'You put your right foot out.'"

He looked down at her. "You put your whole life in and you shake it all about."

Behind them the musician resumed his romantic tempo.

Damon pulled her close and twirled her. "I love trees."

And on a bridge over the Tiber under a Roman moon surrounded by trees they danced and laughed and fell in love. . . .

"I want to grow trees in western Massachusetts," Damon said as their horse-drawn buggy rolled smoothly beneath a canopy of trees through the Borghese Gardens. "The ancients believed that gods dwelled in them."

Gazing up at the trees, she saw that from their vantage point in the buggy the moon was patterned by a green lattice of leaves. It was a mystical sight. "Maybe they're watching us now." She snuggled into him a little. "Do you feel as strongly about shoes as you do trees?"

"Oh, much more. Here"—he patted his

lap—"put your shoe here. I haven't had your shoe in my hand for a couple of hours."

Enchanted by his request she did as he asked.

"It's not just a shoe, you know." He bent his head and addressed the shoe. "You're a foot covering. And you have changed the course of history. Imagine Admiral Byrd exploring the Arctic without his insulated boots. Would Jim Ryun have run the first four-minute mile without a crushproof sole in his sneaker? Would Tina Turner have been the Acid Queen without five-inch platform heels? Where would the world be without you?"

She giggled. "Indoors."

With a smile he gently kissed her instep. "You know Botticelli's *Birth of Venus*? You have her feet."

"I know," she said, amazed that he would know that.

He kissed her foot again, and her expression turned curious. "You do that a lot?"

"Just yours."

"Not even some special foot in Boston?"

Dramatically, obviously teasing, he gazed up at the sky and drew in a deep, meaningful breath.

She playfully swatted him. God, he was

just as wonderful as she always imagined he would be.

The pearlescent colors of dawn were just beginning to streak the sky as the taxi drove off, the driver honking good night to them.

On the porch of the church of Santa Maria in Cosmedin, Damon regarded the *Bocca della Verità* before them, a giant marble disc with the mask of a Triton. His expression was very serious. "The Mouth of Truth. *Roman Holiday.* 'Legend has it—' "

Faith held up her hand. "No, let me say it. First Gregory Peck says, 'Legend has it that if you tell a lie and put your hand there . . .' "

" '. . . it will be bitten off.' "

"Then Audrey Hepburn says: 'Oh, what a horrible idea!' And he says: 'Let's see you do it!' " She looked at him, her eyes aglow. "Let's see *you* do it."

"I have a better idea. Let's do it together. In fact, I dare you."

She lifted her chin, silently accepting the challenge. Tentatively she raised her hand and ever so slowly moved it toward the mouth, and he did the same thing.

Watching each other closely, they inched

their hands inside the mouth. Farther. Farther. Until at last they had their hands all the way inside the mouth.

Damon smiled. "Well, that was easy enough."

"Yeah, it was," she said, going to great lengths to look relaxed.

Then all at once and at the same time they both shouted in pain and pulled out their arms.

Completely dismayed, Damon held up his handless arm enclosed in the sleeve of the navy blue blazer. Faith held up her handless arm, enveloped in the folds of the red velvet stole. They exchanged horrified looks and each screamed.

Damon popped his hand out of his sleeve. "Hello."

Faith pulled her hand out from beneath the stole. "Hello."

Then she held out her hand to him and he held out his hand to her. Faith looked down at their clasped hands. *Two halves of a missing whole.*

7

Damon kept Faith's hand clasped in his as he softly kissed her. They stood on his hotel balcony with Rome spread out before them as the pale gold sky above them slowly brightened. And it felt as if the pulse of the world had slowed and they were the only two people on earth awake at that moment to savor the perfection.

And it was perfection, he thought. He was completely enchanted, captivated. By everything about her—by the nearness of her, by the softness of her curves, by the seductiveness of her scent. She was all red velvet and silken gold skin and everything he had ever wanted without knowing he wanted it.

He didn't want this dawn or this time on the balcony to ever end. He didn't want to ever let her go. And if he had anything to say about it, he wouldn't, because he had the very sure feeling he could kiss her until eternity ended and never grow tired of her.

With a soft little sound Faith broke off the kiss and gazed up at him, her eyes luminous with happiness. "Did you ever feel like you'd been wandering in the desert for as long as you could remember? With nothing but emptiness around you, as far as your eyes could see."

"Only my whole life."

"And then suddenly, when you least expected it, somehow, some way, you stumbled onto an oasis."

He took her face in his hands and stared down at her. Then solemnly, almost mystically, he kissed her eyes, her mouth, her neck.

She sighed sweetly. "I was born to kiss you." She pressed her lips to his face, his mouth, his neck. "Only . . . there's one thing you should know about me."

"Nothing you could say would change the way I feel," he murmured, still kissing her, unable and unwilling to stop.

"Damon?"

"Ummm?"

"I'm . . . engaged. I'm supposed to be married in eight days."

He raised his head and looked down at her. "Nothing except possibly that."

She turned away, her guilt weighing heavily on her. "And he's a friend of yours. It's Dwayne. From high school. That's how I knew you were here. When you called, from the airport." She clasped her hands together and chanced a glance at him. Irrational though it might be, she felt as if she were confessing an affair to him. But he was looking at her with complete understanding and acceptance, and it gave her the courage to go on.

"It just happened. I was alone. And he was . . . there. And I guess I was afraid I'd never find you. But now everything's changed. I owe it to him to let him know. I need to tell him."

"You're sure? You're sure you want to break the engagement?"

"I've never been more sure of anything in my life."

He smiled. "Good."

"Yes," she said, taking his hand. "Good."

He drew her against him again and she went willingly, wrapping her arms around his neck. When he lowered his mouth to hers, she stood on tiptoe, taking his kisses and giving back even more. She felt no awkwardness, no tentativeness. Her body fit perfectly against his. This moment had been predestined in another time. She had dreamed it and now she was living it.

Somehow they made their way into the room to the bed. The kisses were endless, unhurried, sweet, and overwhelmingly irresistible. She couldn't *not* kiss him. It was a compulsion beyond her experience, a compulsion that took her breath away with its absolute rightness.

Sitting on the bed, she leaned back against a pillow and he followed her down, his kisses deepening, becoming more passionate. It was heated madness and passionate sanity. Nothing and no one had ever been so perfect.

But there was one thing she had to do yet. She went still beneath him. "May I use the phone?"

He drew in a deep, uneven breath. "You want to call Dwayne?"

"I think I should. It's only right. Otherwise . . ."

"Otherwise you'd feel like you were cheating on him?"

"You understand," she said, awed by the

way their minds worked together. Perhaps their hearts too. After all, it was fated to be.

He stood and reached down for her hand to help her to her feet, and for a moment his expression was uncertain. Inexplicably this beautiful, enchanting woman had come into his life. Inexplicably, instantly, forcefully, he had fallen in love with her. With hardly a thought he had taken a risk and gone with it. But right from the beginning he had known there would be consequences for his actions, and now he had to face them.

"Faith?"

"Yes?"

Her eyes held such trust, such love. He was frightened. He *couldn't* lose her. "Nothing. Make your call."

"It's going to be all right," she said reassuringly. "It really will."

With a nod, he walked around to the other side of the bed, ostensibly to give her a little privacy but in reality to give himself some space and time to think. What was he going to do?

She picked up the phone and began to dial.

He ran his hand through his hair. *Ah, hell . . .*

"Faith, ah, before you do that, I have a confession to make too."

She paused. "Okay—what?"

He looked at her worriedly.

She hung up the phone and knelt on the bed to be closer to him. "Don't be afraid. You can tell me."

Irresistibly drawn to her, he knelt on the other side of the bed. "You're sure?"

She moved closer to him. "We found each other, didn't we?"

"Yes, we did." He moved closer to her, until very little space separated them. "God, Faith, I don't want to lose you." Unable to stop himself, he reached for her and crushed his mouth down on hers. The kiss was urgent, demanding, and they tumbled to the bed, caught up in the moment and each other. The kiss went on and on, growing stronger, sweeter, continuing until rational thought began to recede and the sensuality was nearly unbearable.

But he had to end the kiss so it could all begin. . . .

Lying on her side, facing him, she tenderly stroked his cheek. "What's wrong?" He didn't answer. "It's all right, this is our destiny. You can tell me anything."

He took a deep breath. "Okay. Okay, the thing is . . . I'm not exactly . . . I mean . . . only in the most literal sense . . ."

"Yes?"

She gently pressed her lips to his, but he couldn't keep the kiss light. She was everything he'd ever wanted. Driven by an uncontrollable need, he deepened the kiss. The depth of what he was feeling for her staggered him, the power of what he felt astounded him. But before he could have her completely, there was something he had to tell her.

"Faith," he said, his tone infinitely regretful. "I'm not Damon Bradley."

It felt to her as if the earth shifted beneath her. *"What?"*

"My name isn't Damon Bradley."

"I don't understand." She hoped she didn't. She prayed she didn't.

"I just told you it was Damon Bradley, but it's not."

The earth fell away beneath her, and she was engulfed by a devastating pain. She leapt to her feet on the opposite side of the bed from him and stared at him, stunned. "Then what is it?"

"It's Peter Wright." He heaved a sigh of relief at the confession. He had done what he had to do to get her. Now there was nothing standing between them. Nothing. He opened his arms for her. "Come here," he said tenderly.

The look she shot him would have killed him had it been a bullet. She snatched up her purse and her stole and headed for the door.

"I'm sorry," he said, scrambling after her. "You're upset, right? But listen, everything else is true. I swear. I'm nuts about hockey. I do live in Boston. I buy Italian shoes for Filene's, Bonwit's, Jordan's. And I'm single. I love trees. But, okay, I admit it, mea culpa—I lied about one little thing."

She reached the door and whirled to face him. "*One little thing?* You call your identity one little thing?"

He stepped in front of the door to stop her.

"Get out of my way!" She grabbed for the doorknob, but he blocked her.

"You said whatever it was you'd understand."

She was hurting so badly she could barely think. She yanked the door open with a force that caught him off guard and he stumbled forward.

"That was before I found out what *it* was."

She ran out the door and dashed down the

hallway. Peter raced after her. "Wait! Let's put this in perspective. You're going to let a few little letters of the alphabet keep us apart?"

At the elevator she jabbed her finger against the button, then began to pace. Her one goal was to get away from him before she broke down. Nothing was making sense to her. She had danced on a bridge over the Tiber under a Roman moon with him and known without a doubt he was the man fate had meant for her. She had believed in him, in *them*. Now she didn't know what she believed in.

"Look," he said desperately, "if the name's that much of a problem, why don't you just call me that? It'll be my nickname."

"How could you do this to me? How could you lie like that?" Tears stung in her eyes, but she was determined not to cry in front of him.

"How could I do it?"

The elevator arrived.

"Can't you see? I did it because *I'm in love with you*!"

She got on the elevator. "Oh, come on, what kind of excuse is that?" She yanked the elevator grate across, shutting the door in his face.

"Faith!"

But the elevator had gone and so had Faith.

D*ear Larry,*

Kate held her pen poised above the postcard as she studied the salutation. So far so good. But now what should she say?

She glanced around the warm atmosphere of the Piazza Margana Restaurant where she was having breakfast. It smelled like freshly baked bread and oranges. Not too far away her waiter, a middle-aged man with a neat little mustache, was drawing her a cup of cappuccino. When he finished, he made his way back to her.

She put down the pen. "So, you're saying you think I should call him?"

He set the cup and saucer in front of her. "He is your husband, no?"

"Yes, but he was having an affair."

"An affair?" He poured a glass of water for her, then looked at her, puzzled. "Yes?"

"The point is, he was *sleeping* with another woman."

"Uh-huh. Yes." He stood there, waiting expectantly.

"They were having *sex.*"

"Ah, now I understand." He nodded gravely. "She was your best friend."

"No. She wasn't my best friend."

He shook his head in sympathy. "Your sister."

"Of course not."

He snapped his finger. "Ah-hah! His first wife?"

"Look, she wasn't a friend or a relative, current or former. I don't know who she is. It's someone I've never met."

Satisfied that he at last understood, he nodded, but then saw that she was still unhappy. *"Ascolta, un sposo discreto e bravo! Molto bravo."*

"My Larry? *Molto bravo?* Because he's discreet?"

"Chiaramente!"

She gave the matter some thought but decided no matter how she looked at the situation, she still couldn't accept it. Exasperated by the waiter's logic, she crumpled up the postcard. "So when does Giovanni get back?"

Just then she looked out the window and saw Faith climbing out of a cab. Good heavens, she looked shell-shocked! She ran out of the dining room in time to intercept her at the stairs. "Faith? What happened?"

"He's not Damon Bradley." Pain glittered in her eyes. "Can you imagine? He just told me that. I traveled all this way and ended up getting involved with an impostor." She started slowly up the stairs. Her legs felt as if they were weighted down by concrete. Her mind felt numb. Her head and heart hurt.

Kate anxiously followed her. "But, listen, at least he was a *nice* impostor."

The warmth of the bathwater soaked into Faith as she lay with her head resting on the rim of the tub and stared vacantly up at the ceiling. But her pain and anger remained.

Kate walked in and handed her two aspirin and a glass of water. "Yeah, sociopaths—they're able to figure out what you want them to be and then they act like that."

She swallowed the aspirin with several sips of water, then handed Kate back the glass. "But how could he know? He only just met me."

Kate set the glass on the floor, then knelt to wash Faith's back. "Men have ways. That's all I know. But it's just so unfair. You meet the man of your dreams and he turns out to be someone else."

135

Faith nodded silently, wishing the aspirin would kick in and take her pain away. But she knew the aspirin wouldn't help. This was a bone-deep pain that confused as much as it hurt.

The vendor at the Campo dei Fiore market added yet another handful of flowers to an already enormous bouquet.

Peter gestured with his hand. *"Molti."*

She obliged and looked at him questioningly.

"Molti."

She tossed in a few more, then started to wrap them up. *"Basta cosi. E bellissimo."*

Peter shook his head. "No. *Molti."*

Kate sat on the side of the bed in their room in the *pensione* and stared at the telephone. She should probably call Larry.

She was so far away from home and everything and everyone truly important to her. On the other hand, there were also problems back home, problems she didn't know what to do about, problems that made her sad and scared. And right now she was extremely thankful for the distance between her and Pittsburgh. This trip had provided a much-needed respite for her. Unfortunately, whether she was ready or not, she would be going home soon.

She should probably check in with Larry. Except she wasn't sure she was ready to face him *or* their problems.

Tentatively she picked up the receiver and dialed overseas.

In Pittsburgh the phone rang in the office at Larry's roofing company. Standing outside in the rain, directing a truck to pull out, he heard the ring and ran inside.

"Larry's Roofing."

No one answered him. He straightened, suddenly alert.

"Kate?" he said softly.

Silence.

"Kate, is that you? Kate? Where are you?"

The phone clicked dead, but he continued to hold the receiver. God, where was she? What was she thinking? He would never have thought his Kate would leave him. He'd always been able to count on her. Always. And he'd always loved her. *Always*.

When had life gotten so complicated? More important, when had Kate gotten away from him? What had he been doing when it had happened? Had he blinked? Had he looked away?

He felt something wet hit the back of his neck and glanced up. Another leak. He slid his coffee mug beneath the drip just as one of his workers walked in.

"Helluva day, huh?"

"Yeah," Larry said glumly. "Helluva day."

Back in the room at the *pensione* Kate lifted the receiver and considered whether she should place the call again. Larry hadn't sounded mad. In fact he had sounded anxious. She couldn't remember the last time she had heard anxiety for her in his voice. Maybe when their second child had been born. No, she didn't think even then. But she had been anxious for a long time now—about him, about their marriage, about their love.

Her thoughts were interrupted by a knock at the door.

When she answered it, she found Peter standing in the hallway, his face nearly concealed by the huge bouquet of flowers he carried.

"Well, well, well," she said witheringly, "if it isn't the great impostor."

He stepped past her and into the room. "Where is she? I have to talk to her."

"She went to get our airline tickets home."

"Home? You're going *home*?" He put the flowers down on a side table.

She eyed him skeptically. He sounded upset, but then, men did when things got a little complicated and stopped going their way. Just as Larry had . . .

"Yes, we're going home. She's going to marry the podiatrist. How could you lie to her like that?"

"Lie?" he said, starting to pace. "I had to stop her—that's how. You know, I wasn't even supposed to be in Rome. My boss was supposed to do this buying trip, and at the last minute he got the measles. The *measles*. Who gets the measles at forty-three? So they sent me. And I wasn't supposed to be in that piazza. I'd gone to the movies, only it wasn't subtitled. Can you imagine a Woody Allen movie dubbed in Italian? So I was wandering around. And then I saw her. And all I know is, when I looked into her eyes, I saw something. I can't even put my finger on what, but something I'd never seen before—"

"Mania."

"Whatever, it matched what I felt inside me. And I thought, please God, give me a sign, give me some way to keep this woman from getting into that taxi and disappearing from my life forever. And He did. She told me the name. Granted, it wasn't *my* name, but it was a start. And if that's not destiny, I don't know what is."

In spite of herself, Kate was touched. "That's really romantic." She placed a consoling hand on his shoulder. "Too bad she hates your guts." She started leading him toward the door.

"It's just a *name*, for Christ's sake. The whole thing is so ludicrous. For all she knows, this guy could be the biggest loser on the face of the planet. He could be a grump, a cynic, a man whose mind is infested with dark thoughts, a criminal. He could be a *criminal*."

Kate shrugged. "It doesn't matter."

"Yeah, but I mean, realistically, what are the odds that this is a terrific guy?"

"Ten billion to one."

There was another knock at the door and she opened it. Giovanni, every bit as tall, suave, and handsome as he had been the last time she had seen him, was standing there with a single rose in his hand. He held it out to her. She looked at the rose, then at him. It had been so long since she had received a rose from a man.

"Kate, I have returned."

The honeyed afternoon light bathed the tile domes and terra-cotta roofs of Rome. From their table at the terrace restaurant, Kate and Giovanni had a breathtaking view, but they were too engrossed in their conversation and in each other to notice.

"So, Larry, that's my husband, he's a roofer, a roofing contractor, but before that, when he was younger, he used to paint. Not houses, pictures."

Giovanni reached across the table and took her hand.

"Ah, but"—Kate nervously shifted in her chair—"you can't raise a family on paintings. Don't you have to be getting back to work?"

Humor and understanding sparkled in his dark eyes. "It's siesta."

"At home only the kids take naps in the afternoon."

"In America, they care for work, they live

to work. They stop for nothing. But in Italy, we care for food, for pleasure, for love."

Beautiful shoes passed back and forth across the runway in front of Peter. As each shoe passed he inspected it and either nodded his approval or disapproval.

"*Sì. No. No. No.*"

A pair of red shoes passed in front of him, and the pen in his hand paused. "*Aspetta. Aspetta!*" The shoe was the Kenneth Cole original of the red shoes Faith had been wearing the evening he had met her.

God, what was he going to do? He might not be the man of her dreams, he thought longingly, but she was the woman of his. And he couldn't let her get away, he wouldn't. . . .

8

As she entered her room in the *pensione* that afternoon, airline tickets in her hand, Faith called wearily, "Kate, are you here?" No one answered.

Then she saw the flowers. They were heaped in a large, colorful pile on the side table—large, fragrant blossoms, small, delicate buds. In fact, every kind of flower imaginable. And she knew without having to be told that Peter had brought them.

Momentarily softening, she crossed to the table and reached out to touch the petal of one flower. He had chosen these for her and they were perfect, just like their time together had been.

She had been so sure Peter was the man destiny had chosen for her. So completely positive. And her belief hadn't been without foundation. Their every movement, their every word, had been perfectly in sync, and their kisses had been inconceivably right.

But his name wasn't Damon Bradley. And because it wasn't, her conviction in herself and in everything she had ever believed was shaken badly. She was left to question the convictions she had held all these years, and to question them was to question herself.

She couldn't ever remember being as confused and as hurt as she was now.

The absolute certainty that destiny had chosen a man named Damon Bradley as her perfect soul mate had been like her own lodestar. Time had passed, and he hadn't come. But still she had tried to wait. And even though she had been days away from marrying another man, when she had heard the name Damon Bradley she had dropped everything and flown thousands of miles to find him.

Except she hadn't found him. It had all turned out to be some ironic cosmic joke.

But there was a question that continued to haunt and confuse her: *How could kisses from the wrong man feel so right?*

Regaining her resolution, she pulled her suitcase from beneath the bed and was unzipping it, when Kate walked in, grinning from ear to ear.

"Hi-iii . . ." she said in a singsong voice.

"Hi. Where've you been?"

"Sightseeing. God, Rome really is the garden of the world."

Faith motioned to the tickets on the table. "I was able to get us out on the first flight tomorrow. Eight A.M." She began to carefully fold her clothes and place them in her bag.

Kate's face fell. "Tomorrow? So soon?"

"The sooner the better. I've been kidding myself. You were right from the beginning. Dwayne is a good catch, *too* good to let get away."

"And what about Peter?"

"Peter? Peter was a mistake." She smoothed her hand over the red velvet dress, the dress she had worn that magical night.

"He was kinda fun though," Kate said wistfully.

She jerked her hand away from the dress. "He was arrogant, boastful, and actually quite eccentric. And not in a good way."

"Like your way."

"Yeah. No. Very funny, Kate. I can't believe I ever kissed him."

Kate's eyes lit up. "I knew it. I *knew* you kissed him."

"What if I did? It means nothing to me now. It's dust. What's that look?"

"You're crazy about him."

"I am not."

"You are too."

"I hate him."

Kate stripped off her blouse and walked to the sink to wash up. "Hate? That's a strong response for someone you said you didn't even like."

"I hated what he did, lying to me like that. And I'm happy I'll never see him again."

Kate dried off and pulled on a black sweater that clung to her body. "Good. 'Cause that's exactly what I told him when he brought over the flowers."

Faith's head came around. "Which one? You told him I hated him or—"

Kate smiled slyly. "Can't stand him, huh?"

Faith turned away. "That's right. I can't." She couldn't remember ever feeling as miserable as she did at that moment, and she wondered if it was remotely possible that she could be coming down with the flu. "Better start packing, I'm arranging for our cab to come at the crack of dawn."

A whistle sounded from down in the courtyard.

Kate ran to the window and waved to Giovanni.

"Katarinnn-na," he called up to her, "*la bella Italia*, she is waiting."

Faith walked over, glanced down at Giovanni, then looked at Kate.

"He promised to take me on a tour of the fountains. But I don't have to go."

Faith's gaze shifted back and forth between Kate and Giovanni, and realization dawned. She yanked Kate away from the window. "You're going out with a guy in an Armani suit and you're wearing a tight sweater! Do you know what you're doing?"

"He knows I'm married," Kate said defensively. She paused. "Besides, Faith, when will I ever get another chance to see Rome from a Roman point of view? I'm learning quite a bit."

Faith gazed at her with knowing, half-lidded eyes.

"We'll be back before dawn. Bye." And like a shot Kate was gone.

Faith stood there a moment, nonplussed. *The whole world had gone crazy.* Worse, she had the terrible feeling that *she* was leading the pack. She pushed her suitcase aside, flopped on the bed, and grabbed the telephone.

A short time later she was listening to Dwayne's answering machine.

Hi, it's Dr. Dwayne Johnson. Don't be a heel, leave a message.

"Hi, Dwayne. It's me. I'm just calling to say I'm coming home tomorrow." Her gaze drifted to the window, where beautiful vivid colors of tangerine and magenta painted the sky, another gorgeous Roman sunset in progress. "The conference has been rather disappointing. I'm skipping the end of it. I'll be arriving on American, flight number 966 from JFK. It gets in at twelve forty-five. So, I'll tell you all about it then."

She hung up the phone and looked across the room, where the garment bag holding the wedding dress hung like a specter on the back of the closet door.

"The sixteenth century exalted the human figure," Giovanni said, pointing to the graceful female figures that were the focal point of the Bernini fountain he and Kate were sitting on. "This was their way of glorifying the human spirit. But it's an ageless preoccupation. The female body has always contained the essence, the mystery of human life."

Kate's joyous laughter rang out over the Piazza Navona that twilight had colored lavender. "I love to hear you talk. No one has ever talked to me that way before."

He brought the back of her hand to his lips for a kiss. "That is tragedy."

"Yes, well," she said ruefully, "it's also my life back in Pittsburgh."

"Someday I will visit you in Pittsburgh and you will show me all her beauties."

She laughed again. "Pittsburgh is nice, but this"—she gestured around the lovely old baroque piazza—"this is beautiful."

"No," he corrected her, and took her face in his hand. "*This* is beautiful."

Kate sighed with happiness. Nothing could ever come of this flirtation, of course, but Giovanni was a much-needed balm to her badly wounded heart and she couldn't help but enjoy their time together. Soon enough it would be midnight, and just like Cinderella, she would be back in the kitchen.

Faith approached the concierge, an old man sitting just inside the doorway of the *pensi-*

one, resting. "Excuse me, but I need to arrange a taxi to the airport for six tomorrow morning."

The old man stirred in recognition. "Ah, yes, *signorina*—Pietro Wright? He left three messages. He calls every ten minutes."

"*Grazie,*" she said with measured politeness. "But no calls for me, *per favore.*"

"Pity." The concierge shook his head and resumed his resting.

She walked outside into the courtyard, where water dribbled from a small elegant fountain of a wistful Venus. A cat ran across her path and disappeared in the shadows. As she watched it go, she tripped over a loose brick.

"Ow!" Balancing on one foot, she held the injured one. "Damn, damn, damn." Stubbing one's toe was an ignominious way to end an Italian holiday, but then, she corrected herself, it hadn't really been a holiday. Not a true one. No, it had been a quest, a foolish quest.

Looking up, she saw Peter coming toward her. She immediately turned and started to limp briskly back toward the lobby.

"You're limping," he said with concern, coming up beside her.

"I know I'm limping. I stubbed my toe."

"Are you okay? You want some help?"

She shied away from his outstretched hand. "No." She couldn't trust herself to let him touch her. She remembered his touches all too well. They had made her feel as if she had never really been touched before and as if there were no other man in the world who would ever touch her again in quite the same way.

"Are you sure you don't want some help?"

"No." What she needed was professional help—Kate had been right about that too.

"You're leaving, aren't you?"

She stopped and turned to face him. He looked tired and upset. In fact, he looked as bad as she felt. She didn't want to hurt him, but by lying to her he had hurt *her*—badly. "If it's any of your business, yes."

"And I suppose you're going back to get married."

"Yes. Everything's already planned."

"To the foot doctor." He looked her straight in the eye. "Why, Faith?"

She averted her gaze. "Because I know who Dwayne is. He's reliable, stable, and honest."

"In other words, he's safe."

"Is there something wrong with loving somebody who's safe?"

"Do you love him?"

"Would I be marrying him if I didn't love him?"

"Do you love him?"

"Will you quit asking me that?" Her foot came down wrong and she winced. "Ow, damn, my toe!" She collapsed onto a nearby decorative stone bench.

"Do you love him, Faith?"

Her toe throbbed with pain, keeping her heart company. "Go away, Peter," she said softly.

He got down on one knee in front of her and took her foot in his hand. "You stubbed your toe, don't you think that's a sign?"

"A sign?"

"He's a foot doctor. Pain is your body's way of telling you something is wrong. Your toe is trying to tell you not to marry Dwayne."

She was much too vulnerable and too confused for this conversation, she thought, pulling her foot out of his hand, getting up, and limping away. "That's ridiculous. My toe is fine. What I need is a new pair of shoes."

He surged to his feet to follow her, but she

turned on him. "Peter. *Stop.* What we had was an illusion. It was an illusion, and we both wanted to believe it, but it was founded on a lie."

"So?"

"It wasn't real. You weren't who you were supposed to be. So I wasn't really who I am because you weren't who you are."

"You were exactly who you are, just as I was. Just as I am. A name doesn't change that."

"You're wrong."

"I'm not wrong. What about the oasis in the desert?"

"That was a mirage."

"Yeah, but I'm the man you were born to kiss. Remember?"

Of course she remembered. She might never forget. "Listen, Peter, I came here looking for something—"

"I know—and you found it."

She shook her head and her expression was infinitely sad. "I don't even know you."

"Get to know me."

"No. You're the man of someone else's dreams."

"I belong in your dreams. Don't throw your life away on somebody you don't love."

"Who says I don't love him?"

Very gently he took both of her hands in his and looked deeply into her eyes. Her eyes were still the most glorious he had ever seen, but they were shuttered against him. He felt defeated.

"Well, then," he said gently, "go home and marry your podiatrist." He brought her hands to his lips and tenderly kissed their palms. "I hope you'll be very happy." Releasing them, he walked quickly away.

She looked down at her hands and her palms that still tingled with warmth from his lips.

"But if you'd like to grab a quick cappuccino instead," he said, coming back, "I'm game. The stars are out tonight. Maybe we could find one of our very own."

She turned her back to him so that he couldn't see the tears in her eyes and mutely shook her head.

He stared at her back, trying his best to think what he could say or do to change her mind. But he had no more words, no more angles.

A minute later she whirled around. "Peter . . ."

But it was too late. He had gone.

And then the tears began to fall.

The day dawned gray and wet. Kate stood in the courtyard of the *pensione*, waiting for the cabdriver to finish putting their bags in the trunk. She hadn't bothered to even put on any makeup. Somehow she couldn't summon any joy for their impending trip home. The truth was, she wasn't yet ready to go back and face the reality of an unfaithful husband and a crumbling marriage.

She hadn't realized it until she had gotten to Italy, but she had been living on the edge of her nerves for a long time. Italy and Giovanni had been good medicine for her. The problem was, she didn't feel healed yet.

As the driver stuffed the wedding dress in on top of the suitcases, she turned and glanced at Faith. "We're ready to go here."

"Be right there." Faith held out a tip to the old concierge. "Thank you for everything."

He shook his head, refusing the tip. "Come back soon, *signorina*."

She nodded, but she knew she would never be back. There was nothing for her here but the memory of shattered dreams. She hurried to the cab and climbed in beside Kate. "Let's go."

As the cab pulled out of the *pensione*'s driveway and into the stream of traffic, a single tear slipped down her cheek. Funny, she thought, she would have sworn she didn't have any more tears left.

Peter suddenly appeared beside the window, running alongside the car. "You can't go!"

She wiped the tear. "Why not?"

"Because I know where Damon Bradley is."

"Stop the cab!"

Minutes later she, Kate, and Peter were walking down the road back toward the *pensione*. She and Kate were carrying their suitcases and Peter was carrying the wedding dress.

"I couldn't sleep last night," he said, still out of breath from chasing after the cab. "I did something wrong and I didn't know how to make it up to you. I was up half the night, so you know what I did? I went back to Sabatini's for a chocolate *gelato,* and I spoke to the waiter, just on the off chance that the waiter knew the name of the guy's hotel. And he did."

"You're kidding!" Kate said, amazed.

"That's right. So I called there, and they said he left yesterday. But apparently he comes here every year, always follows the same route. He always goes from here down to the coast to the Le Sirenuse Hotel in Positano."

"Where's Positano?" Faith asked.

"It's south of here—we can be there in about three hours. Did I do the right thing?"

She had decidedly mixed feelings. If she agreed to go to Positano, she would get to spend more time with Peter, which she didn't think would be such a smart thing to do. She had been too happy to see his face appear in the cab's window. She had been too eager to seize any excuse to ask the cab to stop.

No, it wouldn't be smart. After all, he had tried everything to get her to forgive him, but then turned right around and gone to a lot of trouble to find her soul mate for her. Of course she hadn't given him much choice. . . .

"Giovanni can take us," Kate said excitedly. "He's got a car."

9

Giovanni cheerfully hummed along to the sound of the purring motor of his old and much-loved Ferrari Mondiale as he negotiated the convertible around a hairpin turn that skirted the Gulf of Salerno. "This is one of the most beautiful roads in the world, no?" he asked with a glance at Kate, who was sitting beside him.

"It is, yes," she said, relaxed and happy.

"It is heaven on earth and I am sharing it with an amazing woman by my side and good friends." He beamed over his shoulder at Faith and Peter in the backseat.

Faith couldn't help but smile in return.

The day and the scenery had gotten to her too. Beneath a cerulean sky, sheer cliffs dropped off to silvery rocks, azure seas, and transparent depths. They had passed beneath cliff-hanging villas and above emerald and sapphire grottoes. The sun was brilliant and warm, the air crystal-clear.

Giovanni gestured expansively toward the countryside that was an enchanted land of steep hillsides overgrown with lemon trees, jasmine, and bougainvillea. *"Una bella giornata."*

Kate hung her head out the window and her long blond hair streamed in the wind. "Anything could happen here. . . ."

She had once felt that way, Faith remembered. But in many ways it seemed like an eternity ago rather than just days earlier.

She glanced at Peter. He both baffled and fascinated her. She wished she felt free to reach over and put her hand on his and share what she was feeling about the day and about him.

They had meshed so beautifully, so perfectly, when she had thought he was Damon Bradley. But when she had found out he wasn't, boundaries had moved and foundations had shifted. And ever since, she had been scrambling to try to adjust and understand.

He smiled at her, glints of laughter and warmth in his eyes. "Is this a great day to be alive or what?"

"It is," she said, relenting a little. "It definitely is."

The fact that once again she was chasing after Damon Bradley wasn't as important to her as it once might have been. Something in her had changed. This time her interest in finding Damon Bradley had more to do with satisfying her curiosity than it did with fulfilling a dream. For a brief while with Peter she had experienced what it might be like to find her soul mate, and it had been wonderful. But Peter had been the wrong man. The thing was, that wrong man was occupying a great part of her thoughts.

The wedding dress was draped over the seat between them, puffed up high, and as effective a barrier as the Great Wall of China, but somehow Peter still managed to casually sling his arm behind her back. She had the wildest urge to toss the wedding dress out the window and snuggle against him as she had in the horse-drawn buggy. She viewed the urge as a definite sign that she was still much too vulnerable to him.

She leaned forward. "Giovanni, I have to make an important phone call. They're expecting us in Pittsburgh today." She lightly smacked Kate on the back of the head. "Right, Kate?"

Kate shot her a defiant look. "No one is expecting *me*. I've never called."

"Maybe you should."

Kate gave her a sarcastically sugary smile. "And maybe I shouldn't."

A little farther along the road, Giovanni pulled the car off to the side and pointed. "There's a café, Faith. You can place your call from there while the rest of us enjoy the view."

"Fine," she said, now wishing she'd never thought of the call. But she had given Dwayne her flight information and it would be irresponsible of her not to tell him she wasn't coming back after all. At least not right away.

Kate, along with Peter and Giovanni, climbed out of the car and made their way to the edge of the cliff.

The waves of the Mediterranean broke against the rocks far below them, sending azure spray high into the air. And atop the cliff where they stood, the wind whipped Kate's skirt and hair out around her.

"This is fantastic," she said, exhilarated.

Giovanni's eyes twinkled appreciatively at her. "These are the winds from Africa. They sometimes bring the sands of the Sahara across all of Europe, even to the icy mountaintops of Switzerland."

"And just think, I never knew this place existed until today, and now I'll never forget it."

"Ah, but just wait until we get to Positano. It is a dream beckoning you to come and then return again and again.

Like a little girl, Kate clapped her hands together in excitement. "I can't wait!"

Peter stared glumly down at the water, but when he heard Faith approach, he turned.

"Did you get through?" Kate asked.

"I left a message at his office that we're delayed."

"Delayed." Kate grinned. "I like the ambiguity of that word."

Peter slipped his hands into the pockets of his slacks. "And you didn't give a new time of arrival?"

"No." She couldn't tell what he was thinking. His face and voice were without expression. But then, why should she care what he was thinking? And why should she worry about *why* she hadn't given Dwayne some idea of when they might be coming home? She turned away. "God, look at those rock formations. They're—"

"Beautiful," Kate said, finishing her thought.

"Have you ever heard the story of the Sirens?" Giovanni asked.

Kate shook her head. "No, I haven't."

"Homer talks about them in his *Odyssey*," Faith said. "Beautiful women who would lure sailors to their death with their singing."

"That's right," Peter said, looking at her. "They were seduced by their songs of love."

Giovanni pointed to the rocks below. "They say the sailors, they would tie themselves to the mast, they put wax in their ears, do anything to try to escape them. But year after year, ships were wrecked, lives were lost. This coast, she was covered with the bones of men."

Kate stared down at the rocks, mesmerized by the dangerously beautiful shoreline. "But they weren't real."

Giovanni shrugged. "I guess not." He

paused. "All that for something that doesn't even exist. The things people do for love, no?"

The things people did for love, indeed, Faith thought ruefully. "I think we'd better get going." She turned away from them and walked back toward the car.

Peter picked a wild daisy and caught up with Faith. "Did you love that story?"

He handed the daisy to her and casually put his arm around her. She looked at his arm but didn't say anything.

"I know you loved it. You're a romantic."

She tossed his daisy away. "I *used* to be a romantic, but I'm not anymore."

"Then why did you agree to come to Positano?"

That was a very good question, she thought, reaching the car. It was a shame she was so confused about the answer.

Positano was a picturesque village of pastel-colored moorish-type houses nestled stair-step, one on top of the other against the cliffs, their ocher, saffron, and pink hues muted by time. Lemon and orange trees, along with bougainvillea and oleander, scented the air, and the sea competed with the sky in a contest of unearthly blues.

Giovanni eased his Ferrari to a stop in front of the Le Sirenuse Hotel, an elegant eighteenth-century villa perched above the village and the mesmerizing sea.

"Oh, my God," Kate said, gazing up at the handsome façade of the palazzo. "Joan Collins stayed here."

Giovanni's laugh was filled with appreciation. "Come. You will love it here."

They all got out of the car, and in rapid Italian Giovanni directed the bellhop to their bags and the wedding dress.

Faith entered the spacious, elegant lobby filled with fine antiques and exquisite furnishings. As she had in Venice at the Danieli, she scanned the room in a slow three-hundred-and-sixty-degree turn. But the excitement and expectation she had felt in the Danieli lobby were missing. The anticipation that all things were possible was gone. Now all she felt was a mild interest in the elegant men who were reading international newspapers or business reports and chatting among themselves. Her eyes stopped at Peter's smiling face as he came up to her.

"Giovanni is on his way to the front desk to see about our reservations."

She nodded.

"And he's going to ask about Damon Bradley." He paused. "Good luck, Faith."

"Thanks." What else could she say? When she had agreed to come to Positano, she had committed herself to a certain course of action. She couldn't back down. Besides, it was the right thing to do. She turned away from him, fighting against the surprising urge to cry. Something was very wrong with her. In her whole life she didn't think she had cried as much as she had since she'd met Peter.

Reaching the desk, Giovanni addressed the desk clerk. "I am Giovanni Martini. I have reserved two rooms. One is for myself and Signore Wright and the other is for Signorina Corbett and her sister-in-law. And could you also tell me if Damon Bradley is in his room right now?" Giovanni listened as the desk clerk gave him the information.

Across the lobby Kate walked up to Faith, her expression concerned. "Are you all right, honey?"

Aware of the intensity of Peter's gaze on her, Faith forced herself to smile. "Sure. Couldn't be better." Over Kate's shoulder she saw Giovanni approaching and her stomach knotted with a strange dread. "He's not here, is he?" she asked, vaguely surprised by the tone of hope in her voice.

Giovanni smiled broadly with the air of a man delivering good news. "Right now he is by the pool. He wears a gold medallion."

She was going to be sick, she thought. What was she doing here? She and Kate should have stayed in Rome a few more days. They could have gone sightseeing. Maybe with Giovanni . . . and Peter. *No*, not Peter. "You were right about destiny, Kate," she said softly. "If it was serious about me meeting this man, it should have been more helpful."

After a quick glance at Peter, Kate spoke to Faith. "You don't have to go out there and meet him. We can leave."

Peter's gaze on her was so fixed, so watchful, she had to believe he knew exactly what she was thinking, right down to her very last doubt. Her pride kicked in. "*If* he's really out there, I might as well say hello. After all, I've come this far."

"Sure, why not?" Peter said in a tone that was meant to be nonchalant but somehow fell short.

"I hate men who wear jewelry," Kate said to no one in particular.

As they exited to the pool area that had a view of the town and the beach, Giovanni discreetly hid his small gold chain inside his shirt.

The sun shimmered off the water in the pool and reflected on the men and women who lounged by the pool sunbathing or sipping cocktails.

Aware of being closely scrutinized by Peter, Kate, and Giovanni, Faith dutifully scanned the crowd until she found a man reclining on a lounge chair, a glint of gold around his neck.

She started her survey of him at his feet, which, she couldn't help noticing, didn't reach the end of the chair. He had hairy legs. *Really* hairy. He also had a pot belly and, sure enough, a gold medallion rested on his even hairier chest. But on his head he was losing hair. Faith's face fell.

"Aren't you going to go introduce yourself?" Peter asked with a little smile.

"Of course I am." She took a hesitant step.

"Wait." He reached out to gently brush something off her blouse. "Lint," he said softly.

She looked up at him, immobilized by the intimacy and tenderness of his touch.

"Do you want me to go talk to him for you?" he asked, his voice as gentle and as intimate as his touch had been.

"No. I came all this way to see him. *I'll* talk to him.

She cast another look at the man on the lounge chair. *Rats.* He was still there. She swallowed hard and walked slowly over to him. "Hi . . ."

His eyes were closed. She cast a look back at Kate for support. Unfortunately Kate was frowning. "Uh-hem, excuse me. Hello . . ."

He cracked one eye and squinted at her. "You're in my sun."

"Oh, sorry!" Flustered, she hopped out of the way.

He closed his eyes again.

This meeting—supposedly a monumental event in her life—wasn't exactly going as she had once imagined, but then, nothing else had either. "Pardon me, but . . ."

He squinted at her again. *"What?"*

If she had ever felt more like an idiot than at that moment, she couldn't remember. "Uh, do you have the time?"

He looked her up and down, his expression clearly indicating he thought she was some sort of curious life form. "Do I look like I'm wearing a watch?"

He was barely wearing a bathing suit, only one of those thin little strips of spandex Europeans seemed to think was a good substitute.

"No, I guess not. I just thought maybe—"

"Damon!"

At the sound of a little girl's voice calling out *the* name, Faith swung around just in time to see a glittering god shoot up out of the water in the pool, sending a sunlit crystal spray of water droplets out around him.

Faith gasped. The man was no ordinary mortal. He was a living monument to mankind. In fact, he could have modeled for Michelangelo.

He climbed out of the pool and began to towel off, and Faith couldn't take her eyes off him. His hair hung in lustrous dark curls around his handsome face to his shoulders. A halo of sunlight glistened off his tanned, muscular body, and his deep brown eyes were warm and seductive. *And* a small medallion, delicately carved in gold, rested in the hollow of his powerful chest.

A few discreet meters away, Kate's gaze shifted to Peter and eyed his suddenly crestfallen expression with sympathy.

"Wow," Giovanni murmured beside her.

"Bye, Damon!" the little girl called, waving. "See you *domani*!" Her father wrapped her in a towel and led her away to the elevators.

Beside the pool, Faith grabbed hold of a nearby chair as her knees started to give way. "Damon?" Her voice was barely audible, she realized, and tried again. "Damon *Bradley*?"

The bronzed god spoke. "Uh-huh."

"Excuse me."

Damon tossed a towel around his neck and looked at her.

"Hi . . ."

"Hello," he said, perfectly friendly.

Faith nervously fingered her necklace. "Beautiful place . . ."

"Sure is."

At the outdoor bar a mandolin player quietly began to strum a romantic Italian tune, throwing Faith off guard. The ambience was right for this long-imagined moment, and the bronze god was *more* than right. So why did everything seem so wrong?

Determinedly she tried again. "Been here long?"

"Just since yesterday."

"I just got here too. Not yesterday. But just now. Today. Just a few minutes ago." She glanced around, wishing she could think of something truly intelligent to say, but her mind had gone blank and there was not even one stray intelligent thought to be found. "Yeah, we just got here. That is, me and my sister-in-law. My brother's wife."

He looked at her. "Uh-huh."

She couldn't do this, she thought, losing her nerve. There was no point to it anymore. "Well, listen, I'll probably be seeing you around, then." She began to ease away from him.

"I hope so," he said, his tone polite.

Faith stopped. What was she doing, walking away from a god? His polite reply had just presented her with a window of opportunity, and Peter and Kate and Giovanni were going to think she was crazy if she didn't at least *try* to see him again. She turned back to him.

"I was wondering—" He was rubbing baby oil on his perfect pectorals, and the sight so distracted her she had to look away for a moment. "Uh, do you have dinner plans?"

He popped on his sunglasses. "Tonight?"

"Um, well, *any* night."

"Well, not exactly . . ."

Lord, this was embarrassing. She had to fight against the urge to slink away. "Would you be willing to have dinner with me?"

A slow smile crept across his sensual, perfectly shaped lips. "Sure."

"You would?" she asked, maintaining her cool with difficulty. "Really?"

He nodded, and behind him Faith saw two bikini-clad women subtly check him out as they passed by. She didn't blame them. It wasn't every day a person saw a sun god in sunglasses. "Okay, good, okay . . . uh . . . where?"

"How about I meet you at Il Covo del Saraceni. It's the restaurant at the bottom of the stairs at, say, eight-thirty?"

"Il Covo del Saraceni. Eight-thirty." There. It was done. A great sense of relief swept over her and she gave him a smile that would melt Nome in January.

He eyed her smile with interest. "I'll look forward to it."

She began backing away. "Okay. Good. See you then, then."

He held out his hand in warning. "Be careful. You're about to trip over that lounge chair."

She stopped just as the back of her knees hit metal. "Oh, thanks."

"Aren't you going to tell me who you are?"

"Oh, Faith." She stepped forward and held out her hand. "My name's Faith."

"It's a pleasure to meet you, Faith. See you tonight." He shook her hand, then turned away.

"Tonight," she said, and hurried toward her friends. Giovanni and Kate were smiling broadly. Peter looked exceptionally unhappy. And right at that precise moment she couldn't face any of them.

They thought she knew what she was doing. All three had gone out of their way to help her. She didn't want them to know how uncertain she felt. Especially not Peter. She dashed past them and straight into the elevator.

The sound of hammering could be heard across a series of asphalt rooftops in Pittsburgh. Larry, hammer in hand, nails in mouth, nailed another shingle into place. But at the sound of his cellular phone ringing, he stood, spit out the nails, and pulled it from his crammed utility belt.

"Hello? What? Just a minute." Unable to hear, he walked to the edge of the roof to get as far away as possible from the other workers, who had kept up their hammering. "Okay . . . that's right. My wife used her card yesterday and I can't remember the amount she told me. No, I can't wait for the statement." He paused, listening. "Uh-huh, uh-huh, and an approval for four hundred from Le Sirenuse Hotel in Positano? Italy? My wife's in *Italy*? What the hell is in *Italy*?"

Suddenly he realized everything was quiet, and he looked around to see his workers staring curiously at him. "Get back to work," he growled, and hung up the phone.

Damn. He couldn't remember ever being as miserable as he was at that moment. What in the hell was Kate doing in Italy anyway?

Kate gazed raptly at Giovanni as he translated a plaque on the wall of the Villa Cimbrone.

"Here, in the spring of 1938, the divine Greta Garbo, escaping from the clamor of Hollywood, shared with Leopold Stokowski hours of secret happiness."

"Sharing hours of secret happiness," she murmured. "Who would have thought I'd have so much in common with Greta Garbo?"

10

Laughing softly, Kate pirouetted around the hotel room, sending the full, calf-length skirt of her new black dress flaring gracefully out. She had bought it that afternoon in an elegant shop on one of Positano's tiny, twisted lanes. The dress had thin spaghetti straps topped by a deep garnet stole that draped around her and over her arms. The whole effect was soft and romantic and matched perfectly how she was feeling.

She ended her impromptu dance at the window, leaning on its sill. Beyond the window the sun was slowing sinking into the indigo sea in an indescribably beautiful sunset.

Coming to Italy had been one of the best

things she had ever done for herself, she reflected. She was feeling stronger and more whole than she had in a long time.

"Did you see Damon's eyes?" Faith asked behind her. "*Bedroom* eyes."

Kate turned to see her sliding into a slip. "He probably wears tinted contact lenses."

"No, but honestly, he was really nice."

"Who are you trying to convince?" she asked, and received a glare as her reward.

"No one."

"That's good, because no one in this room is buying it. Not me, and certainly not you."

"Kate—"

"Just tell me one thing, why are you doing this?"

Faith grabbed her brush and looked at it. Finally unable to remember why she had picked it up in the first place, she put it down again. "Doing what?"

"Going out with this Damon?"

"God, Kate, you of all people should know why. He's my destiny."

She sighed. "Faith, sweetie, you've got an extremely bad case of tunnel vision."

"Damon Bradley is here, isn't he? The Ouija board spelled out his name. Madame Divina said his name. And now I've met him and I'm about to have dinner with him. That sounds like destiny to me."

"That's all true, but there's something else that's true too. It's like you're forcing yourself to stay on course even though there's an excellent possibility that you should have turned left back in Rome."

Faith stared at her for several moments. "Yeah, well, I did turn left for a little while and lived to regret it."

"Maybe, just maybe, you should have kept going with that left turn, at least for a little while longer."

She sighed. "I don't know. It's like I've been involved in this weird game that started when I was nine and I've been waiting for it to end ever since. Well, now it seems that I've almost reached the end of that game and I have to see it through. Don't I?"

"I don't know. I guess, if you say so." She glanced back out the window. "God, look how the sun sets over those hills. Larry would just love the roofs."

"Ah, so you *do* remember the name of your husband."

"That's never been a problem. *Him* remembering *mine* is another matter though." She absorbed Faith's worried look. "Listen, this trip is like a moment out of time for me. We'll be going back soon and then I'll have to face my problems. But until then I want to enjoy every glorious moment of *now*, because it's very likely that this sort of magical time will never happen to me again. You do understand, don't you?"

Faith slowly smiled. "Pursuing magical moments? Yeah, I guess I do."

Kate relaxed again. "So how old do you think Giovanni is? No more than forty, right?"

"Uh—" There was a knock on the door. Faith grabbed a robe and slipped into it. "Come in."

Giovanni opened the door and stepped in, but when he caught sight of Kate he stopped dead in his tracks. "Oh, Kate, the stars will be jealous of you tonight. You are a vision."

She laughed delightedly. "*Wow.* Do you ever know how to talk!"

"Hey, hey, hey, keep that door open." Peter's voice came to them from somewhere down the hall and moments later he appeared in the doorway, carrying a box. Without waiting for an invitation, he walked right in and sat down on the bed.

And Faith couldn't stop looking at him. He was incredibly handsome, dressed casually

179

stylish in his navy blazer—the same one he'd worn that first night they had met—along with navy slacks, a crisp white T-shirt, and white tennis shoes.

Kate started out the door. "*Arrivederci*, Peter. See you later, Faith."

"A moment," Giovanni said. "I invite you all, on your last evening in Italy. My friend has a yacht, you can see it from the balcony. I told him I would bring all my American friends tonight. You must all come."

"Yeah, thanks, great," Peter said enthusiastically. "We'd love that, huh, Faith?"

With a wide, meaningful smile directed at her friend, Kate waved to her. *"Ciao!"*

And then Kate and Giovanni were gone and she was left alone with Peter, the wrong man who had seemed so right.

She had made a huge left turn that night in Rome, one that had left her shaken to her core, and she still hadn't recovered. She supposed tonight's dinner with Damon was her way of trying to reassert normalcy in her life. After all, Damon—or the *idea* of Damon—had been a normal part of her life for years. Peter was the aberration.

She pulled herself together. "We'd love that, Peter? *We?*"

He shrugged. "I mean, in another lifetime, or a parallel universe, we'd have loved that, right?"

"I gotta get ready," she said, and bolted into the bathroom.

He rose and knocked on the door. When she opened it a crack he handed her the box he had been carrying. "This is for you."

"What is it?"

"You'll see."

She shut the door and in a few moments yelled in delight, *"Shoes!"*

Peter wandered over to the dresser where her makeup was spread out. "They're bone. The perfect color for a rendezvous with destiny. And don't worry, they'll fit perfectly." He squirted some of her perfume into the air and inhaled it. It was lightly floral, feminine, and sexy—like her.

"They do," she called from the bathroom. "Thank you."

"You're welcome." He pulled her dress, hanger and all, off the back of the closet door and held it up in front of him, imagining her in it. It was a long, slim white column of a dress, cut away at the shoulders and back. He swung the dress around and watched as it glided lightly through the air. She would look like a dream in it. *His* dream. But she was going to be wearing the dress with another man, a man any woman would find attractive.

He supposed most people would think he was crazy for putting himself through the torture of being there, but he couldn't not be. As long as he and Faith were both breathing, there had to be a chance for them. He couldn't accept otherwise. The guy might be a hunk, but he was counting heavily on her not liking him once she got to know him. After all, looks weren't everything. Were they?

"Could you hand me my dress?" Faith called out. "It's on the closet door."

He took the dress to the bathroom door and passed it to her, then went back to the dresser and searched through a small pile of costume jewelry. He picked up a pair of gold earrings, looked at them for a moment, then rejected them. He selected another pair that were small, delicate pearl teardrops. Holding them up to his own ears, he studied them in the mirror, then nodded with approval.

"Earrings!" Faith called from the bathroom. "The pearl teardrop ones."

He smiled, then grabbed up a delicate gold anklet and went to the door and handed her the earrings.

"Oh, and could you get my"—he handed her the anklet—"oh, thanks!"

He stepped out onto the balcony. She was so convinced that destiny had chosen a man named Damon Bradley. What if she were right? But no, she couldn't be right.

He was as sure that he and Faith belonged together as she was sure that she belonged with Damon Bradley. He wouldn't be putting himself through this evening if he weren't. He wouldn't be taking the chance.

He tapped his foot impatiently. God, he wished the next few hours were over with.

He heard the bathroom door open and turned to see her standing there in the white dress. Just looking at her left him breathless.

He wanted to take her in his arms and kiss her until she wouldn't have the strength or the desire to walk out the door. And after the time they'd spent together in Rome he was convinced he would be able to do it. But he didn't want to get her by coercion. He wanted her to understand—as he did—that they belonged together, name or no name.

Except watching her go out with another man tonight would be the hardest thing he had ever had to do, and he wasn't quite sure how he was going to make it through the evening.

Finally, he broke the awkward silence that had fallen between them. "You look great."

"Thanks." Nervously she cleared her throat. "Peter, I just want to thank you for making this all possible."

"It was the least I could do. I hope tonight you find what you're looking for. It's going to be"—his lips curved into a sexy smile and he took her hand and twirled her—"some enchanted evening . . ."

"Stop."

He drew her closer, unable to resist after all taking her in his arms. He dipped her and their mouths were very close.

"Stop it, Peter," she whispered, emotion clogging her throat.

"I wish it was going to be you and me tonight."

"I have to go."

Reluctantly he lifted her until she was standing again, but he kept his arms around her. "No matter what happens tonight, I love you."

She stared at him, stunned. And remembered. Just before she had gotten into the elevator that night in Rome, he had told her he had lied to her because he loved her. She'd been so upset, she supposed the hurt over his lie had blocked out the statement. If she'd given it any thought, she would have viewed the proclamation as another blatant lie to get her to forgive him. But he seemed serious now, and in many ways it disturbed her even more than his lie.

"Don't say that."

"Why not? It's the truth."

"I don't want to hear it."

"You don't have to hear it, Faith, because in your heart you already know it, don't you?"

"No, I . . . have to . . ."

"Yeah, I know—it's pumpkin time."

He had never felt more frustrated in his life. If it were possible, he would physically rearrange the universe so that the stars were aligned into a giant arrow that pointed straight at him. Maybe then Faith would realize he was the man for her. Instead, all he could do was grind his teeth together and sweat out the coming hours.

Faith descended the stairs, her sheer white chiffon wrap floating out behind her, making her look like an exotic butterfly.

Each step she took brought her closer and closer to her destiny. She should be happy, excited. But all she felt was tension and dread.

Damon was waiting for her at the base of the steps, completely dry and dressed for their evening out in an ensemble that reminded her eerily of the seventies—a really outdated white jacket, white pants, and an open-necked white shirt.

As soon as the traitorous thoughts occurred to her, she hastened to correct herself. No, he was just an offbeat personality, that was all. Someone who wasn't a slave to fashion. And he still looked like a young god, her Adonis.

"You look like a goddess," he said, and reached for her hand.

He was perfect, she thought, taking his hand. Really perfect.

Every inch a gentleman, Damon pulled out a chair for her at Il Covo del Saraceni, an open-air restaurant overlooking the sea.

With a fixed smile on her face she sat down. "This is a wonderful place."

In fact, it was a setting straight out of a fantasy where moonlight glistened on the water as waves crashed to shore and night-blooming flowers released their sweet fragrance into the air.

"I was hoping you'd like it." He settled himself across from her, and when a waiter materialized at their side, he asked, "Wine?"

"Yes, thank you, I'd like that."

"Brunello di Montalcino, '85, please." After the waiter left, Damon leaned forward. "I know this probably sounds crazy, but I noticed you out at the pool even before we spoke. I could sense a chemistry between us."

"Really?" She had dreamed this moment, and everything was just as it should be. She was in an incredibly romantic setting with the man who was her destiny, and he was gorgeous. Except . . . The moment was perfect, but she was not a part of it. She felt awkward, detached. She had to keep trying, that was all.

The waiter reappeared and poured their wine. Faith waited until he had left, then lifted her glass in a toast. "Well, to . . . new friends."

"And more," Damon said in a deep, meaningful tone, clinking the rim of his glass against hers.

"So, uh . . ." *No matter what happens tonight, I love you.* Peter's words came back to her, interrupting her train of thought. She had to scramble to remember what she had

been about to say. "So, uh, I guess you're
wondering why I asked you to dinner."

Damon set his glass down. "Not really. I
happens to me all the time."

She laughed awkwardly. "Yes, I imagine
that it does."

*No matter what happens tonight, I love
you.* The words hammered at her brain. She
hadn't had to try with him, she remembered
They had talked and laughed. And they had
kissed and kissed and kissed.

Damon picked up his menu and scanned
it. "Son of a bitch! Look at these damn
prices!"

Faith was taken aback by his outburst
but recovered quickly. "Don't worry about it,"
she said graciously. "You're my guest." She
picked up her menu. "What looks good?"

Damon perused the menu. "Hmmm . . .
well, the scampi sounds good."

"You like shrimp?" she asked, reaching
for the tiny sign of compatibility. "*I like
shrimp."*

*No matter what happens tonight, I love
you.*

"Small world," he said, lifting his wine
glass again.

"Small world," she agreed wistfully.

On a beach on the boardwalk below the elevated restaurant, Peter anxiously studied Faith and Damon through his binoculars. They were sitting against a wrought-iron railing, and with the help of his binoculars he could see them clearly. Unfortunately he couldn't *hear* them, and it was driving him crazy.

But he could see every smile Faith gave the guy. Once or twice she even laughed.

Damn, he had hoped she wouldn't have a good time. In fact, he had counted on it.

Forlornly he glanced at his watch. God, this was the longest night of his life. What were they doing up there anyway? How long did it take to eat a meal?

He reached for his bottle of wine, *his* dinner. They were probably dining on lobster.

A wizened old man with a huge cane made his way over with a slightly unsteady gait and sat down to take a breather from his evening outing.

Peter spared him a brief glance, but then returned to his scrutiny of the pair. Damn, he couldn't stand to see her smiling like that at the guy. She had the greatest smile. He turned back to the man beside him. "Hey, do you believe in destiny?" The old man didn't even look at him. He must be hard of hearing, he decided. "Do you believe in destiny?" he asked in a louder voice.

"*Non parlo inglese,*" the man said grouchily.

"*Il destino? Capisce?* Understand?"

"*Ah, sì. Il destino . . .*" He raised his cane heavenward and pointed up to the stars. "*Tutto il mondo cree nel destino.* It is written"—his English was broken—"stars . . . everywhere."

The moon had laid down a path of light across the blue-black waters of the harbor and the elegant, gracious yacht rode at anchor in the path's shimmering light. On board the party was at its height.

But at the bar, Peter drank alone, morosely watching the other guests dance and stroll along the deck, every one of them having a good time.

Where were Faith and Damon?

Once again he searched the crowd and found instead Kate and Giovanni standing at the bow, chatting.

"Kyle, he's in the third grade, he's the

smart one," Kate was saying. "My other son is very physical."

Giovanni pressed a finger to her lips and leaned toward her until they were very close. "You think I'm just one of those men who tries to seduce every woman he meets."

"I know that's what you are," Kate whispered.

"Does it matter?" he asked, his voice a whisper also.

No, she thought, gazing up into his hypnotically dark eyes. It didn't. Because at this time in her life he was exactly what she needed—a suitor, someone to court and woo her and make her feel that she was the most precious object on earth. Larry had once made her feel that way, and it was a wonderful feeling. She knew it wasn't realistic of her to expect the feeling three hundred and sixty-five days of the year. But every once in a while, like now, it was very, very nice.

He kissed her, a soulful, passionate kiss, and she responded, soaking up the romance of the moment and the heady feeling of a handsome, unattached man desiring her.

"There are beautiful teakwood cabins below. Would you like to see one?"

"I . . ."

At the bar, Peter tensed. Faith and Damon's motorboat had just arrived. As he watched, Damon put his arm out to Faith and pulled her gracefully onto the deck and they climbed the stairs and strolled to another part of the bow.

"I told you everything about me," Faith said, her smile still fixed firmly in place. "I want to hear about you. What poems do you like, what novels do you read, what kind of music do you listen to?"

Damon wrapped his arms around her from behind and she melted back against his warmth. He was really very nice, she thought, still trying.

"I like action movies," he said, speaking slowly and seductively into her ear. "Steven Seagal movies."

"Ummm . . ." Steven Seagal? she thought. His movies were so violent and stupidly macho. About to voice her opinion, he nuzzled her ear so tenderly, she forgot her objection.

"I read Hemingway."

Hemingway was good, she thought. *Where was Peter?*

He kissed the nape of her neck. "I like bullfights."

She frowned in disappointment. How could he like bullfights? The bulls suffered so. He nuzzled her other ear so gently, she almost gasped. "Music?"

Through the constant movement of the partying crowd, Peter kept a close eye on Faith and Damon, and he was getting more and more upset. Damon was making moves on her that were way out of line.

"I like everything," Damon was saying in answer to her question. "Michael Jackson. Frank Sinatra. Madonna. Except opera." He nuzzled her neck.

"Opera? You don't like opera? I'm surprised to hear that because"—he put his hand on one of her breasts—"hey." Casually she brushed his hand aside, deciding to act as though it had been a mistake. "Ah, excuse me—um, tell me about theater."

He placed his hand on her other breast. She turned to him. "Please, that makes me uncomfortable." To her astonishment, he reached for her again. She pushed him away. "I said stop!"

Unfazed, he grinned. "That's what you want."

"It is *not*! Stop it!"

Damon reached for her again. Angry now,

she put her hands against his chest and pushed as hard as she could.

Suddenly Peter appeared between her and Damon and threw a hard right punch, hitting Damon in the face and sending him flying to the deck. He sprang up and, unable to stop himself, Peter went after him again. He'd had all he could take this evening. His nerves were shot and any tact he might have had was long gone.

Down the railing, Giovanni kissed Kate's face softly. "There is no floor beneath us. No roof above us . . ."

With a regretful sigh, she pulled back from his kisses and cupped his face in her hands.

"What?" he asked.

She smiled tenderly up at him. "Oh, Giovanni, you are so gentle and kind and beautiful. And I'll never forget you. But I'm married. And I can't do this."

He pulled her closer to him and gazed deeply into her eyes. "My beautiful Katarina . . ."

God, but it was hard being good, she thought ruefully. Where was the harm of being bad for just a little while longer? She threaded her fingers up into his hair and kissed him passionately. He made her melt, he made her forget.

Somebody ran past them, brushing against them. Then more people ran by. And more. Kate and Giovanni broke apart and turned to see Peter and Damon struggling together. Giovanni immediately rushed to restrain Peter, and Kate dashed to Faith's side.

"What happened?" Kate asked.

Anxiously Faith watched Peter, worried that he might be getting hurt. "My Adonis turned into pond scum."

"What're you doing, Peter?" Damon yelled, lying on the deck, holding his bloody lip. "That's how you repay a favor? You *told* me to turn her off!"

"I didn't tell you to grab her. I didn't tell you to *molest* her."

"*What?*" Faith felt *she* had been hit. This couldn't be happening again. Had she really fallen for another fake? Was she really that foolish? That stupid? "What did you just say?"

Peter turned to her, his hands out in appeal. "Listen, Faith—"

She looked at the man lying on the deck. "You mean you're *not* Damon Bradley?"

"No," he said, rubbing his jaw, "my

name's Harry. And I'm telling you, Peter, that was the last time I'll ever do you a favor!" Angrily he snatched the wig off his head and hurled it to the deck.

Stunned, the crowd gasped at the sight of his completely and utterly bald head.

For a moment Faith thought she might faint. Her knees went weak and her head whirled with dizziness.

It *had* happened again, she thought in shock. Peter had lied to her and tried to manipulate her, not once, but *twice*. He was so adroit at juggling the truth, she wasn't sure of anything anymore. Once more he had pulled the rug out from under her, and this time she had hit bottom hard.

"Let me explain. *Please*, listen to me."

She couldn't think, couldn't look at him, couldn't stay there one more second. "Come on, Kate, we're out of here." She dashed down the steps that led to the bottom deck and then the next set of steps that led to the landing for the dinghy.

With a wave to Giovanni, Kate followed. "Good night."

Giovanni's smile was charmingly regretful. "*Buona notte*, Katarina."

Peter ran after them. "Wait! I had to do it! You were leaving!"

Faith and Kate jumped into the dinghy, the motion causing waves to slap against the hull.

Peter stopped above them on the first deck and leaned over the railing. "Faith! I was afraid of losing you. I had to try something."

Barely keeping her balance, Faith stood in the unsteady boat and yelled furiously up at him. "I hope you're happy. Start the motor," she snapped at the fascinated sailor who was manning the dinghy. "Kate, sit down. I hope you're very, very happy. Start the goddamn motor!"

Dutifully the sailor started the motor, making her balance even more precarious.

Kate held out her hand to her. "Faith, sit down. You're going to tip us over."

Peter ran down the steps to the landing platform.

"You've ruined everything," she said, shouting at him. Dammit, let's go! You ruined my life. I don't believe in *anything* anymore. I don't believe in the stars, the moon, or the sun. I don't believe in destiny or magic or any of that stuff."

Peter leaned out and attempted to reach for her. "I can *explain*."

The boat heaved, forcing Faith to sit. "I'm going home and I hope to God I haven't screwed up my life. Maybe I can sit down with Dwayne and we can still work things out and be happy together." She turned her ferocity on the hapless sailor. "Would you please *move* it!"

The dinghy took off and at the same time Peter reached for her again. *"Faith!"* He lost his balance and fell over the rail into the water. With a powerful kick he resurfaced in time to see Faith zipping away. "You're gonna miss me when I'm gone!" he shouted. He went under again, and when he resurfaced, his voice was a whisper. "I'm sure as hell gonna miss you."

Giovanni hurried down the steps to him. "Hang on, Peter. I fish for you!"

Slowly Faith and Kate walked up the hillside stairs above the Amalfi harbor promenade. At the top Faith stopped and looked back once more, studying the tranquil beauty of the night through a sheer veil of tears. The moon had begun to wane, but the stars still twinkled brightly against the black velvet sky. And with lights strung from bow to stern, the distant yacht looked like a jewel sparkling in the darkness.

"Faith . . ."

"Oh, Kate, you were right to have doubts about coming to Italy. We never should have come. I'm sorry I dragged you here."

Tears sprang into Kate's eyes too. "Oh, please don't be sorry. Because it's been the most beautiful weekend of my life."

"I'm glad."

"You didn't mean all that, did you?" Kate asked. "About not believing in the moon and stars and—"

"I don't believe in any of it anymore."

"And the part about marrying Dwayne?"

"How can I? Everything's changed. Nothing's the same." The tears spilled over and flowed down her cheeks. God, was she ever going to be able to stop crying?

Kate put her arms around her. "I think *we* were meant to be. You and me."

Faith hugged Kate. "I think you're right."

"Sometimes life is not how you imagined it would be," Kate said a bit sadly.

"Sometimes? How about all the time?"

"Yeah," Kate said quietly. "I'll go pack."

Alone, Faith gazed up at the magnificent stars. How could anything so beautiful be so treacherous?

The party was over and only a few stragglers remained on the yacht. Peter, along with Giovanni and Harry, the second fake Damon, were sitting on the deck in an alcoholic haze.

Giovanni gestured toward the stars. "They come out every night. There's just as many women and just as many promises to break."

"What's he talking about?" Harry asked, his bald head shining as he passed the nearly empty whiskey bottle over to Peter.

"There's just one woman, Giovanni," Peter said forlornly. "And she's crazy. And she's *gone*."

Giovanni placed his hand over his heart and sighed dramatically. "Ah, to almost love a woman. Then lose her." He paused to savor the feeling. "Enjoy the pain, my friend. It's like losing at roulette. There is a sweet sting. Oh, the sweet sadness."

His bald head cocked to the side in wonderment, Harry stared at Giovanni.

"Yeah, well, I'm an American," Peter said,

and passed the bottle to Giovanni. "I hate to lose."

$\mathbb{F}$aith walked slowly into the hotel lobby, each step she took an effort. She was exhausted, mentally and physically. She wasn't even sure she had the strength to make it up to the room, and her mind felt as if it were filled with nothing but the color gray. But there was one more thing she had to do before trying to get some sleep.

She made her way over to the concierge, who was the only other person in the lobby besides a porter, who was vacuuming. "I need to send a telegram."

He waved his hand toward the counter. "These are the cables here."

She pulled one to her and began to write, and as she did, tears washed down her face.

At this point in time it's impossible for me to go through with our wedding.

"Are you all right?" the concierge asked, genuinely concerned. He had a daughter about the same age as she, and he didn't like to see his daughter cry either. "Can I get you something?"

"It's all right. I want to send this right

away." She began to cry in earnest. "I'm calling off my wedding."

The porter shut off the vacuum and moved to another spot, but the concierge motioned to him to stop altogether.

The porter glanced at Faith, who was leaning heavily against the counter, weeping, then exchanged a knowing look with the concierge. Quietly he set about coiling the cord to the vacuum.

The concierge collected the cable, and Faith was left alone to cry and to hurt and to wonder if anything would ever be all right again.

The early morning sun was golden and warm as Kate stood in the drive of La Sirenuse, waving good-bye to Giovanni and Peter. She hated to see them go, but she knew it was time.

Just as the Ferrari disappeared from sight, a taxi drove up and a man got out, carrying a small suitcase and wearing a rumpled tan all-weather coat. He had longish brown hair and blue eyes and sported a night's growth of beard.

Flabbergasted, Kate stared at him. *"Larry?"*

"Kate!"

"What are you doing here? Oh, God, are the boys all right?"

"They're fine. I checked with your mother before I left home."

"Then what are you doing here?"

"That's what I want to ask you!"

"You came halfway around the world to ask me what I'm doing here?"

"No." He drew in a deep breath. "I came halfway around the world to tell you that I love you and that I've missed you like hell."

As wonderful and as magical and as romantic as the sights and experiences had been in Italy, she didn't think she'd ever seen anything more wonderful, more magical, more romantic than Larry standing there.

He dropped his suitcase and she ran to him. "Oh, Larry. I missed you too, honey!"

"Thank God." Larry scooped her into his arms, hugged her against him, and started up the hotel stairs.

"Wait a minute. What about . . . ?"

"What?"

She *had* to ask. "Is there another woman?"

He looked at her as if she'd lost her mind. "Another woman? Where did you get a crazy idea like that? Didn't you hear me? I love you, Kate."

With a sigh of happiness she settled her head on his shoulders. "Oh, Larry, you have to see the view. You can see all the roofs in Positano from our room."

"*You're* all I want to see for the rest of our lives."

It was the most romantic statement she'd ever heard, she thought happily.

"Y ou sure you're going to be okay?" Kate asked Faith sometime later, watching with Larry as Faith zipped her suitcase shut.

She smiled. "I'll be fine, and I really want you guys to stay and have a great time."

"We will," Kate said, giving her a hug.

Faith turned to her brother. "I'm really glad you came."

"Me too," he said, hugging her. "I just wish you were happier."

"Everything happened for the best. Really. Now I know for sure that marrying Dwayne is the wrong thing to do. What if I hadn't found out till after the wedding?" She gave him a smile meant to reassure. "Let's go get me a cab."

"**D**amon Bradley?" Larry's mouth dropped open. "That's why you're here? Kate, *I'm* Damon Bradley."

"*You're* Damon Bradley?" Kate asked with disbelief.

"No, no, I mean the Damon Bradley of the Ouija board." He sat back for a moment while the waiter served them wine and cheese. "God, honey, it was a joke. I was *pushing* the arrow and making it say Damon Bradley. I wanted to get to the next question."

She gazed at him with amazement. "Are you saying you just made the whole thing up? That the guy never existed?"

"Oh, he existed all right. He was a kid I knew from Little League. He was a real jerk. God, I guess Dwayne went to high school with him."

"But what about the fortune-teller?"

"I slipped her two bucks."

She sat back, stunned. "You gotta tell Faith."

"Are you kidding? I *can't* tell her. She called off her wedding. She'll never speak to me again." He took a sip of his wine.

"She's called off her wedding 'cause she's in love."

"Why would she call off her wedding if she's in love?"

"Because," she said quietly, "it's not Dwayne."

"What? Who's she in love with?"

Peter was used to airports. They all had bad lighting and were always crowded, and Leonardo da Vinci Airport in Rome was no exception. But as he stood in line to check in for his flight at Alitalia Gate 40, he was too tired to notice much of his surroundings. He felt completely wiped out, all his wits and energies depleted.

More out of habit than interest, he examined an attractive boot a middle-aged woman was wearing. "Are your boots Spanish?" he asked the wearer.

"How'd you know?"

"They're very nice. Very nice leather. How much did you pay for them?"

The woman gave him a dirty look, but he had already turned away, too weary to care about her answer or her expression.

Outside Leonardo da Vinci Airport, Faith, engulfed in depression, slowly got out of her taxi and dragged herself and her suitcase to the curb. Even the air felt heavy, pressing down on her, making every movement an effort.

"Signorina . . . scuzi, mai . . ."

Faith turned to see the driver walking toward her, holding up the garment bag with the wedding dress in it. The garment bag's zipper had somehow slipped down a fraction and a bit of lace and net were sticking willfully out of the bag. She gazed at it dully. God, that thing had been like an albatross around her neck.

"Buona fortuna," the driver said with a smile, and handed it to her.

Faith nodded dispiritedly. "Right."

Minutes later she stood in a crowded line at Gate 10. The line slowly moved up, and as it did she pushed her suitcase forward with her foot. Her wedding dress hung on her shoulder, as heavy to her as a bag of rocks.

Suddenly a female voice came over the public address system. *"Mr. Damon Bradley, please come to the information desk. Mr. Damon Bradley."*

Faith's head snapped up.

At the same time, in another part of the airport Peter's head also snapped up.

"Signore Damon Bradley, please come to the information desk," the female announcer

said, this time in Italian. "*Signore Damon Bradley*."

Faith's brain clicked into action. *Peter.* What was he up to now? Damn him, hadn't he done enough? Couldn't he just leave her alone? Oh, hell.

Unable to help herself, she moved out of the line, and laden down with her bags she slowly headed for the information desk. As she walked she began to pick up her pace and go faster, faster.

Dashing from the opposite direction, Peter pushed his way through the crowds of departing travelers.

Faith arrived at the information desk at the same time as Peter, almost sliding into him. "What are you doing now?" she asked suspiciously.

He spread out his hands in an innocent gesture. "Hey, I had nothing to do with this."

Just then they heard the attendant on the desk speaking to the man who was standing in front of them with his back to them. "Miss Rexer will meet you directly at your hotel in Geneva."

"Thank you," Damon Bradley said.

Peter reached out and tapped the man's shoulder. "Damon?"

"Damon?" asked Faith, doing the same thing at the same time.

He turned, a professional man who could have easily been a model for *GQ*. He glanced back and forth between the two of them. "Yes?"

Faith couldn't think of a thing to say.

Peter held out his hand. "Damon, hi, I'm Peter and this is Faith. She has been looking for you all her life. As a matter of fact, I think she wants to marry you. Are you married?"

"No," Damon said good-naturedly.

"Good. You have a job?"

Damon smiled, amused. "Of course. Who are you?"

"He's available," Peter said with a glance at Faith. "You see, Damon, she thinks you two were meant to be."

Damon smiled broadly, clearly enjoying the joke. "Oh, really?"

"Only problem is . . . I love her. I love her more than she'll ever know. But you're a lucky man, because you've got the right name. I hope you'll be very happy." With a last look at Faith he turned on his heel and left.

The female announcer came over the public address system. "*Last call for boarding Alitalia flight 409 nonstop to Boston.*"

Disturbed, Faith stood on tiptoe, trying to see Peter through the crowd, but he had disappeared.

"What's going on?" Damon asked.

"Ah . . . he, he . . . loves me." She paused as the full impact of what she had just said hit her. "God, he loves me really very much."

"I can see that. I guess the question is—do you love him?"

"Last call for boarding Alitalia flight 409 nonstop to Boston."

"What?" Faith asked, having a hard time hearing him and an even harder time keeping her mind on what he was saying.

"I said the question is—do you love him?"

The announcer came back on the public address system, this time in Italian. *"Last call for boarding Alitalia flight 409 nonstop to Boston."*

"Do I what?"

"Do you love him?" Damon asked, yelling above the announcement.

She looked up at Damon and then off to where Peter had vanished. And slowly she began to smile with quiet revelation. "I think I do. I do, Damon. I do."

He glanced at his watch and with a smile he handed her his card. "Well, I've got a flight to catch to Geneva. If you ever want to talk this over, here's my card. I operate out of Chicago." He picked up his bag and then with a wave he was gone.

Absently Faith dropped his card into an ashtray. "God," she said quietly. "I do love him."

She took off, walking faster and faster, and suddenly she started to run, down the corridor, through the crowds. Her bags weighed her down, making her clumsy and uncoordinated. A few times she inadvertently used the bags as battering rams, and more and more of the wedding dress escaped from its bag, fighting for freedom.

She arrived at the gate just as a short-skirted attendant closed the jetway door. God, she thought, it was like some horrible déjà vu. Except this time she couldn't have cared less about the buttons on the flight attendant's uniform and she knew exactly who she was chasing. Peter. *She loved Peter.*

"Nonstop to Boston?" she asked breathlessly. "Is it still here? It's leaving. I have to get on that."

"I cannot stop a plane," the attendant said, eyeing the wedding dress, then glancing at a nearby male attendant.

"Please," she said, half crying, half laughing. "You don't understand. The man I love is on that plane."

Several members of the cabin cleanup crew were standing nearby, talking amiably, but hearing her, they stopped and one of them, a man with a mustache and a cap, began to translate to the others what she had just said.

The male attendant walked over. "Are you sure?"

"Yes!" She wiped her tears. "He's going to Boston. Is that plane going to Boston?"

The short-skirted attendant asked one of the cleanup crew for their headsets and she spoke quickly and sharply in Italian into it.

Inside the plane an Italian copilot listened intently to the message coming through his headphones, then placed a hand on the shoulder of the pilot. *"Aspetta un momento."*

The attendant took Faith's ticket and handed a new one back to her.

Outside, an old man who was a ground-crew member talked to the short-skirted attendant by headphone and smiled broadly. *"Per l'amore."* He waved to the other ground-crew member to swing over the mobile steps immediately.

The attendant grabbed Faith's arm and

pulled her down a narrow corridor. A man stood guard at the door at the end. The attendant yelled at him in Italian and he pushed the door open.

Faith rushed toward the light, then, once outside, took off toward the plane.

The male attendant came running behind her with the wedding dress, its whole length flapping rebelliously free in the wind behind him.

The stairs swung into position. She grabbed the gown and ran up the steps.

The attendant with the short skirt waved. *"Buona fortuna!"*

"*Viva l'amore!*" the old man called.

The passengers in the plane peered out the windows at her. The cabin door burst open and a smiling flight attendant waved her in. "Congratulations! Ticket please."

A murmur of confusion ran through the plane. People stood up to see what was happening. Kids darted up and down the aisles. Another flight attendant tried to calm everyone.

Peter tiredly rubbed his eyes and looked around. My God, what was wrong now? Why couldn't the damn planes run on time anymore? All he wanted was to—

"Faith," he whispered in disbelief.

Faith saw him across the crowded plane. *"Peter!"*

He stood, and they met in the middle of the aisle.

"Are you sure?" he asked. "What about—"

"You. Only you." Her eyes were shining with happiness. "A wise lady by the name of Madame Divina once told me that we make our own destiny. Well, I'm taking her advice. I chased after true love and I found it. *You.* Peter, you are my destiny, and thank God I realized it—"

"Just in time," he finished for her, and with a laugh of sheer joy he pulled her into his arms and kissed her with all the passion and love he had in him.

"Please take your seat now and prepare for takeoff," the flight attendant said.

Peter drew Faith down with him into the closest pair of empty seats and kept kissing her. And he didn't stop. Even when the passengers started to cheer. Even when the plane taxied down the runway, gathering speed. Even when the plane took off into the sky with a mighty roar.

Award-winning author Fayrene Preston has written over forty novels for Bantam, most recently *A Baby for Daisy*. She lives in the north Texas area.

Screenwriter Diane Drake is a native of Los Angeles and earned a bachelor of arts degree from the University of California at San Diego. Before turning to screenwriting full-time, Drake held the position of vice president creative affairs for director-producer Sydney Pollack's Mirage Productions.

DON'T MISS
THESE CURRENT
BANTAM BESTSELLERS